WON'T BE THE DEBT OF ME

ORLA
KELLY
PUBLISHING

BY
DEREK O'LEARY

Orla Kelly Publishing,

27 Kilbrody, Mount Oval,

Rochestown, Cork.

Acknowledgements

Families are an essential part of everybody's life. Their presence, or absence shape the people that we become. I am not self-made. My family made me and I am grateful for each of them in my life.

Maureen my mam, Eamon my father. My sisters Claire and Jennifer. And my nephew and god son Max.

To my wider group of family and friends.

Whether you have been in my life briefly or for a long time, you have had an effect on who I have become.

Thank you all.

Contents

Chapter 1:

Another Day

It looks like an ordinary teapot. A little bit tacky, if I'm honest. My mother had one of those, or maybe my grandmother. Possibly my old Auntie May? I couldn't remember exactly, but I'm sure I've seen one just like it before. Charlie stared, eyes glazed.

The teapot appeared familiar to many, due mainly to the fact that it was so mundane, so unoriginal. It looked like almost every other teapot Charlie had ever seen. It was a sun-stained creamy colour. It had browned time-patches. The white patches showed the pot's original colour before the tea stains and the time stains had seeped through. Three quarters of the way down the pot were two blue stripes. They wrapped around tightly and the brush strokes were still visible from an old painter, long since retired. The two blue lines stood an inch apart with a line of chickens in between. Each chicken was identical in size, shape and stance. Chickens queuing up, one behind the other, each leading the way and at the same time chasing its leader's tail. A three- dimensional and hand-painted version of these chickens sat on top of the lid. This chicken was clearly the pick of the bunch and she knew it. She had held her stance and stare for years.

"BANG!"

The sudden loud thump jolted Charlie from his daydream. He once again realised where he was as a warm breeze crossed his face. It crept in from the large open door at the end of the hallway, to Charlie's right side.

"BANG BANG BANG!"

"ORDER!…Going once - twice - sold!"

The auctioneer's voice echoed around the crowded hall. Unusually high-pitched, the voice now began listing the details of the next item, the stained chicken teapot.

How could someone know so much about a teapot? Why did so many people care about a teapot? Charlie scratched his chest.

"What a priceless item!" the man with the hammer guaranteed the crowd. Priceless and other such compliments were the general tone amongst the odd-smelling crowd. Tobacco and wine mixed with that damp clothing smell only found in old tweed. There was so much tweed. Tweed jackets, tweed hats, tweed everywhere. Were they giving tweed away on the way in?

A large gentleman sat at an impossibly small timber table. His knees skimmed the underside of the table top. The wooden top was almost green in colour and seemed to be held up by the man's legs. The table top was empty, save for the base unit of an old telephone, the receiver of which hung on the large man's ear. Every so often the large gentleman would raise a little card with a number on it, a different number every time.

'BANG!'

The hammer demanded the room's attention. A little man stood, struggling to see over the podium on which he persistently pounded his little brown hammer. His lips moved in a vibrating manner. He slid from one word to the next. He sang a mumbling song of numbers as the smelly tweed wearers shouted, pointed, nodded and poked in his general direction.

The crowds' voice grew louder as different individuals pulled on their ear lobes, touched their nose tips, lifted their hat rims or lowered their glasses.

'BANG!'

The little man's small brown hammer was becoming an almost familiar sound. This time its echo was followed by a silence, as the crowd took a deep breath and held it.

I don't envy anybody taking a deep breath in that smelly damp hall.

"Sold for the price of 3 million euros to the bidder on telephone line two!"

The little man with the hammer pointed the little polished tool at the taller gentleman with the telephone hanging on his ear. The crowd gasped and began to talk amongst themselves as a tall white vase with a pale blue pattern was produced and placed where the chicken teapot had previously been. The cacophony of voices hushed to a murmur just over Charlie's shoulder as he turned his back to the auction hall.

"One hundred and fifty thousand, do I hear...?"

3

Charlie scratched his head. He twirled a little piece of his short black hair around his finger.

Three million still doesn't look like much. I'm still sure my ma had one of those.

He scratched his firm chest through his navy overalls. These things don't get half itchy in this heat. The old hall, the sight of the tweed army combined with the heat, made Charlie scratch everything. Sometimes he'd scratch when he wasn't itchy, with the thoughts of the tweed against his skin. He stepped away from the noisy hall then stopped. The sweeping noise his baggy trousers made on the polished hallway floor stopped him in his tracks. He adjusted the shoulder straps on the dusty overalls.

What fecking size did he get me?

Charlie used all his twenty six years on earth to develop and maintain a six-foot-tall athletic build. Apparently white decorator's overalls were only available in two sizes larger than him.

"What happened to your eye?"

Charlie turned, to try to match a face to the phantom voice. A young lady dressed in what Charlie considered an older woman's clothing, stood leaning against the wall. She had 'nipped out for a cigarette.' The click of her lighter sent a quiver into Charlie's shoulders.

"My what?"

"Your eye...what happened to it?"

"I fell when I was a kid."

He rubbed a tiny scar on his jet black left eyebrow.

"Suits you...Adds character to your face and it doesn't distract from your handsome looks."

The stranger lifted the cigarette to the very left corner of her mouth. Her expensive red lipstick stained the cigarette a pinkish colour. She blew a thin film of grey dead flames from the right corner of her mouth. Charlie tilted at the hips slightly. He leaned away to lessen the impact of the charcoal aroma on his lungs.

"Thanks, I think."

Charlie struggled to breathe and speak.

"Don't mention it, handsome."

The lady departed, dropping the now pink cigarette butt.

"Look after yourself."

She stepped on the butt. With precision she used the sharpest part of her shoe heel to quench the smoky plume. She looked Charlie up and down, from his boots to his tanned face and, raising a pencil thin eyebrow, she walked back to the auction hall. Charlie watched her walk away to the heel-toe tune that only high heels can sing. He woke from the high heel-induced daydream when the heat of day fell on him once more. A bead of sweat trickled from his forehead to his cheek, by way of the bridge of his nose.

It was a midsummer's day and, unusually for Ireland, the sun was beaming. It had been for the last four weeks straight. Charlie's skin, born and raised in Ireland, could not take anymore. He had been looking forward to spending this week working indoors, away from the evil sun. The thoughts of being able to hide in the shadowed hallways of Whyte's Auction House, 38 Molesworth Street excited Charlie.

"Charlie, Charlie.......Grab that! Grab that!"

The sudden shouting in the quiet hallway startled Charlie. He spun on his heels. His rubber-soled boots squealed in reluctance to turn. Charlie faced the familiar smile of Paul Sticklen, twenty-six years old and paper thin. His long slim figure held an ounce of awkward for every inch of his height. He stood an impressive six foot eleven inches tall. On top of this neatly stacked column of skin and bone sat a fistful of scrunched-up blonde hair.

"Charlie!"

Paul struggled to carry a massive brass candlestick.- well, one end of it - as Charlie had by now grabbed the heavy end.

"Thanks, Charlie" the relief of a having a helping hand was visible on his face.

"Be careful with it, will you, Sticks."

Sticks was what Charlie called Paul. With a surname like Sticklen and a body frame like a girl guides' camp fire, Charlie deemed Sticks an appropriate calling card from the day they first met at the age of nine.

The two friends struggled with the weight of the large brass candlestick. In tandem they navigated their way down the empty hall. The high ceilings echoed and exaggerated each huff and puff they made. Once out the large door they descended the old stone steps. Together they placed the candlestick onto the loose gravel driveway next to where their van was parked.

Charlie could smell a brassy aroma on the palms of his hands.

"Careful with it" Charlie seemed to always end up being the figure of authority.

"Careful with *it*?"

Sticks looked at the antique and scratched his blonde curls. "Exactly, what is *it*?"

Paul Sticklen was not the smartest of Charlie's friends. However Charlie always knew his heart was in the right place. A little naive and very easily led, but Charlie knew he always meant well.

Charlie considered Sticks one leg of his tripod. The third leg was a Mr William Henry Olsen the Third. If Sticks represented one end of a spectrum William Henry represented the exact opposite end. William had only one possession bigger than his name and that was his belly. He stood broad in the chest and even more so around the gut. William Olsen or 'Old Bill' as his friends had come to calling him had been chubby all his life. Although it had never bothered him.

"We're all built, the way we're built. Can't change things like that. So don't let it bother you."

When he spoke, Old Bill's voice came from within his large chest, guarded on both sides by his mountainous shoulders. As if he wore sporting pads under his shirt all the time. People say chubby people are always bubbly. Old Bill finished every sentence with a smile. An easy smile to remember as more often than not his teeth were glazed with a slimy film of black. Old Bill loved black liquorice. This left him with his signature alien-like smile and a distinct liquorice aroma. Old Bill was the oldest of the three friends.

It might come in handy to know a big older boy in the school yard.

Little Charlie, had approached Bill one day during playtime. Charlie in fact became the first kid in the school yard to approach Bill. Usually they ran away. Charlie explained his 'business proposal' to Bill. Bill had used his mass and girth to tally a collection of sweets from all the smaller kids, every morning. Charlie's proposal consisted of Bill simply handing over some of his sugary loot to Charlie. Charlie would then sell said sweets back to the kids at a cheaper price than the local shop, and then split the money with Bill.

Charlie would set up shop every morning at the outside school gate of Saint Mary's National School. He would sell the masses of sweets they had previously owned back to his school mates. Little did these school mates know that Bill would be waiting at the inside gate of the school, at the top end of the walkway. Bill would stand ready and waiting to collect his candy bribes in return for not imposing wedgies. At first Bill didn't want any part of it, until Charlie explained he would continue to get sweets to eat and could make some money on the side.

8

Money he could use to buy whatever he wanted. Of course at ten years old there's not much else for a boy to buy other than more sweets.

That was Charlie, he always had a scheme, a scam. He was a sure-fire ideas man, but so much more. He could apply these ideas to real life. Sticks and Old Bill had been cogs in the wheels of Charlie's plans ever since that tender age. All the way up through primary school, on into senior school and through many years of tedious odd jobs. Charlie's most recent scheme took the form of an antique transport and distribution company.

Old Bill sat with his knees bent up in front. The van's side step sat lower than usual while holding his weight. It put him in a yoga inspired position, whereby his knees were as high as his chest. His swelled belly sat between his spread legs and hung lower than the rusty step on which he sat. His face looked as if he'd spent the morning hanging upside down. The fresh sweat stains on his shirt explained the musty smell.

"What do you mean, what is it?" Old Bill wiped his forehead on his shoulder.

"It's a large eighteenth century candlestick" Charlie put a stop to any possibility of an argument.

"Must be time to pack it in now?" Old Bill wiped more sweat patches onto his shirt.

"Pack it in? You said you'd have my back for as long as I was doing this?"

Charlie took Old Bill's outstretched hand and helped him up.

"No, not the company! Pack it in for lunch!" Old Bill struggled with his airflow.

"Jesus! I thought you were telling me you'd had enough."

Charlie got a lungful of Old Bill's steamy aura as he pulled him off the step with a clenched fist.

"Four years of this business and I haven't jumped ship yet. I'm not going anywhere at this stage."

Old Bill placed his stubby short thumbs into his pants and hoisted them upwards.

"Thanks be to Jesus, the thought of my Dad coming back from the grave to chastise me is not what I need right now."

Charlie spread his arms and wrapped Old Bill close to his chest. He reached around Old Bill's large warm shoulders and patted his back twice. Two deep thuds.

"He's proud of ya, regardless of whether or not you keep this company going." Old Bill smiled once their embrace ended.

Charlie looked at Sticks struggling to get the brass candlestick into the van. Sticks managed to do so without causing damage to the antique, the van or himself.

"Come on, you. Take a rest, we've done enough. This fella smells like he needs a break and you could do with a rest, too."

Charlie gestured for Sticks to come over, using nothing but his neck. Sticks threw his gangly frame from inside the rear of the van out onto the grey dry stones.

"Lead the way. We'll let the big fella put his feet up before he ends up with another hernia."

His six-foot-eleven-inch frame aided his reach for the van's rear door, which opened up level to the roof. With one swift pull downward, Sticks slammed the door shut.

Chapter 2:

∿

Lunch time

'TING TING TING'

The tea bag spun within the old half-cleaned cup. Brown spirals were introduced into the creamy-coloured liquid as the teabag lived and died.

"That's the biggest load we've done in a long time."

A bead of sweat ran down the bridge of Old Bill's strawberry-like nose. A threefold movement wiped Old Bill's forehead, wiped his sweaty rum nose then raised his sandwich to his mouth, like a choreographed routine.

The load had consisted of old dusty paintings whose solid wooden frames were carved with a scalpel's precision. Swirly flowers and whatnots on every corner. Some furniture reminiscent of the props room of a Hammer horror movie, walking sticks whose owners where long gone, shiny oak hat-stands as thick as the trees they were carved from and, of course, large brass candlesticks. Whatnots of extremely varying values, all of which needed to be moved to the next auction house.

Sticks' cheeks struggled to hold in all his food as he shook his head. A single piece of lettuce managed to escape

12

as far as the lap of his trousers. Charlie sat in the driver's seat of the old van.

"What are you nodding at, that's definitely the biggest load in all the years."

Bill sounded certain, as he put an end to his rambling with another monstrous mouthful of his sandwich.

"We've moved bigger" Sticks said, finally swallowing enough of his food to answer Bill.

Charlie tilted the sun visor in front of his face. A bank-issued white envelope stuffed with several letters fell onto his lap. He somehow managed to ignore its existence for a moment. For one moment, he looked peaceful. He separated himself from the importance of the letter-stuffed envelope, and from the pointless arguing going on to his left within the messy cab. A tiny scruffy cross held Charlie's eye, from where it sat on the underside of the sun visor. Charlie closed his eyes and joined his hands.

"Shut up you, always disagreeing. You were the same last night when I was trying to sleep." Bill used his deep voice to chastise Sticks.

"What? Well excuse me if I'm not into going to bed at nine o'clock!" Sticks squealed back at Old Bill in a higher pitch than his usual.

Charlie opened his eyes and quickly grabbed at the tiny passport-style photograph, which sat squeezed behind the cross on the underside of the sun visor. Bill dropped his shoulders and lowered his sandwich to his lap.

"I don't mind a little bit of music but your music is so…. so repetitive. And why so late?"

"Late? I'm not eleven years old anymore. It was nine o'clock." Small pieces of lettuce escaped from Sticks' mouth as he spoke.

Charlie kissed the photograph and, as quick as he'd taken it down from behind the visor, he shoved it back in, behind the cross. Old Bill began to smirk.

"Keep it up and I'll kick you out."

Sticks' jaw chomped up and down, pounding his food faster than ever before. He quickly swallowed.

"Kick me out? It's as much my house as it is yours. I'll kick you out! You wouldn't really kick me out, would you?"

After much preparation Charlie opened his red tin lunch box. The latch sprung open and echoed around the small cab of the van.

"You two sound like a married couple"

Charlie took a bite. Sticks reached into Charlie's lunch tin and grasped an orange.

"I've got the orange, the apple is yours, big boy."

Sticks grabbed the apple from the corner of the tin and handed it to Old Bill next to him. Charlie finished chewing his first bite.

"When are you going to get your own oranges?"

Sticks' nostrils narrowed and both his bushy eyebrows tilted down at their ends.

"Ah don't be like that. This is *my* orange. She throws it in there for me. She knows I like my oranges and she knows we don't have someone to pack us a pretty little lunch box every day."

Old Bill's belly shook as he giggled.

"It's true. She loves us as much as she loves you" Old Bill added.

"I know she does."

Charlie took another bite. Sticks nodded his head towards Charlie on his right.

"This fella is giving out about an orange."

Charlie finished chewing with a gulp so loud they all heard it.

"Twenty-three years of oranges."

Sticks pushed his lips together and began struggling to dig the orange from its skin.

"Yeah but Katie *always* packed them for me."

"Katie didn't pack my lunch in primary school! And you were robbing my oranges back then, too!"

The smell of orange quickly dominated the squashed cab, as a mist of juices rose from Sticks lap.

"Yeah, well, your Mam - or whoever packed it back then - they packed the orange for me, and Katie packs it for me now."

"Hope you choke on your orange!"

Charlie quickly took another bite from his neatly-stacked ham and cheese lunch. Old Bill shook the van with his giggles. Charlie joined in, laughing.

"There's no need for that!"

Sticks smiled and pushed a soft piece of orange between his lips.

"What's the envelope?" Sticks managed to ask between segments of orange being shoved into his mouth.

"Nothing, that's just a reminder." Charlie took the envelope and quickly pushed it into the glove box.

"Reminder?" Sticks paused to chew a little more, before he tried to continue.

"What's it?"

Old Bill cut Sticks' sentence short by pushing the point of his elbow into his friend's side.

The second Charlie was not looking, he pursed his lips together shaking his head at Sticks, before declaring:

"Hey Charlie! Does she ever ask you did you enjoy your orange? No, but I bet she asks did you enjoy your sandwich! You see, she knows *he* eats it."

The inside of Charlie's lunch box held his eye.

"Yeah, she knows."

***

"Good afternoon, it's two o'clock….."

The radio broke the silence.

"The minister for finance has described the repossession of houses, from families unable to meet mortgage repayments, as *one possible solution*. Speaking today after it was announced, more than 50 families a day are removed from their homes around Ireland. He also said…"

Charlie raised his head from with his newspaper.

"Right, back to work."

Charlie disappeared out of the van and ran into the musty auction hall. Sticks began to collect the wrappings, which had held his and Old Bill's lunch, from the space between the dashboard and the windscreen.

"Always the fastest hour of the day." He rustled the wrappings into a large ball. Old Bill woke up, with all of the banging Sticks made whilst tidying their makeshift food court.

"Is Charlie gone back in?" Old Bill stretched off his nap.

"Yeah" Sticks opened the glove compartment and removed a wet wipe from a little barrel full of them. He quickly wiped the dashboard's surface. The envelope stuffed with letters fell out onto the floor. Sticks noticed the bank's name and address, as he picked it up to put it back.

"Listen, you don't be asking Charlie any more questions like the ones you were asking earlier." Old Bill rarely spoke so softly.

Sticks remained quiet. Whilst looking at Bill he closed the glove box.

"Charlie is a good lad. He'll be ok. He has this all sorted, so you don't be worrying."

"Yeah" Sticks nodded.

"We'll just work harder. We'll just put the head down and work through it."

"I'm sick of it. I'm sick of lifting, sick of breaking my back to earn…..what! Just enough to get by, I'm sick of it." Bill voiced his usual back-to-work protest. Sticks smiled.

"I know, buddy, but we're halfway there, might as well finish now." Sticks brushed any remaining evidence of lunch from his T-shirt.

Old Bill poured himself from the passenger seat. He moaned, and his joints sounded like an old wooden bridge.

"Halfway there. Now, do you mean halfway through the day or half way through this labouring?" Old Bill finally fully removed himself from break position, as he planted his two feet on the grey footpath.

"The day!" Sticks opened the rear of the van.

"Good, because I don't think I could do this for another five years."

Old Bill placed his hands on his hips and proceeded to lean backwards, as far as his bulging belly's counterbalance allowed. His shirt lifted slightly, allowing his belly button to poke out into the open for a brief second.

"You don't see yourself doing this for another few years?" Sticks scratched his head, regardless of the fact that it was not itchy. His hair made a rustling sound as he ran his skinny fingers through his blonde locks.

"Well…" Old Bill quickly replied, paused, and then finally finished "…I never really thought about it. I haven't exactly got a plan for the next few years. Or at least any plans I've ever had, I've abandoned. Plans don't really work out, ya know?"

Sticks' shoulders slumped downward as he cast his eyes to the sundried concrete pavement below his feet. Old Bill threw his large arm around Sticks' feeble frame and rocked him back and forth.

"Don't worry, I'm not going anywhere. When I say I hope I'm not doing this in the next few years, I mean I hope none of us are. I hope we're off, away, living it large on all the millions we're going to make!" Old Bill smiled, presenting Sticks with a perfect view of his liquorice blackened teeth. Old Bill's ever-present aroma was accentuated by such a visual. Sticks mirrored his friend's smile.

"Millions, you say?" Sticks felt the weight of Old Bill's big arm across his shoulders.

"Yeah! Millions! And you know what that means? It means we better get to work!"

The red removal van was visibly lower in the back than at the front, like an abandoned seesaw.

The rear step now sat no more than a few inches higher than the gravel driveway.

***

"Lean back a minute will you Sticks?" Charlie hung his neck left and stretched forward, as the van reached the end of the gravel runway. Creaks and moans sang from the old van's rear shocks, as it began to move off again, out of the gate and to the left.

"*National Arts and Artefacts Society of Ireland, established 1981.*" Sticks read aloud from a shiny brass plaque, which sat housed in the centre of a large marble rock. The marble was almost hidden amongst a plethora of colourful flowers.

"Yes. National Arts and Artefacts Society of Ireland, established Nineteen-Ninety-One!

Thank you, for yet another long and hard day's work!" Old Bill joked.

"Eighty-One." Charlie said, lowering the radio volume.

"Until next time!" Sticks saluted the marble rock as it got smaller within the van's rearview mirror, a foot in front of his tired face. Old Bill opened the glove box and removed a bag of liquorice. Sticks swallowed, to clear the dusty dry feeling from the back of his throat.

"Remember earlier?" Sticks folded his arms, catching sight of the letter.

"How, earlier? Earlier today, earlier in life, earlier when?" Old Bill's tone of voice never changed, and he kept his eyes on his paper.

"Earlier today, when you said about all the millions?" Sticks leaned to his left, slightly closer to Old Bill, while remaining focused on the front windscreen.

"Yeah, what about it?" Old Bill's steady tone rang once more.

"Do you think we'll ever be millionaires?"

The van came to a sudden stop as the bright red traffic light demanded. The red bulb sat so close to Charlie's driver's window that it lit the entire cab. Charlie looked across Sticks to Old Bill.

"Have you been winding him up again?"

Old Bill's response was drowned out by the rustling sound as he turned the page of his newspaper. Sticks shifted in his seat.

"No, he hasn't been winding me up. I was just thinking. Seriously, do you ever think we'll make it? Do you think we might ever achieve all those things we promised ourselves back when we were in school?"

Charlie steered the van away from the lights when the red glow turned emerald green.

"What are you telling me, you're not living the dream?" Charlie joked.

Sticks just shook his head in silence.

"Don't worry, buddy." Charlie gently slapped down his dusty hand onto Sticks' knee.

"We'll make it. We will, I promise. We just have to wait for our opportunity to arrive. God knows it's due anytime now."

Charlie squeezed Sticks' knee slightly. Sticks fidgeted in his seat.

"Yeah?"

"Yeah." Charlie rustled Sticks' sandy hair with his non-steering hand.

Sticks interlocked his skinny arms in front of his chest then leaned back in his seat. Old Bill, once again, turned a page in his paper as he blew a breath out through his nose, which made a noise like a steam kettle releasing pressure. Three deep lines appeared on Sticks' forehead as he placed his left foot onto his right knee.

"Charlie?"

Charlie glanced at Sticks and immediately returned his eyes to the road.

"About that."

"About what?"

Sticks took a breath before starting again.

"About what you were saying. We have to wait for our opportunity to arrive. How will we know the opportunity when it arrives?"

"We'll know." Charlie's eyes again darted to Sticks, then back to the road, as if watching a tennis match.

"Well, I think I might have the opportunity."

Old Bill decided now was the time to add his sixpence: "Yeah? I can't wait to hear this."

He folded his paper in half.

"An opportunity I might know about." Sticks finally finished.

Old Bill's expression never flickered with any emotion, as his eyes examined every inch of his scrawny friend.

"Oh yeah, what's that?"

Charlie's tennis match continued.

"Last week when you had that thing, Charlie" Sticks' voice crackled from the back of his throat.

"Yeah." Old Bill began to smirk slightly.

"Yeah."

Charlie blessed himself almost too fast to be seen by the human eye.

"So, while Charlie was in with the doctor, I'm sitting in the waiting room..." Sticks' crackly voice continued. "I'm waiting, reading Oprah magazine, having already read every magazine in the room at least ten times. You know, the usual, as you do. There's an auld lady here, auld fella there, coming and going, passing complaints and plans for the day."

"Did some old lady offer you her life savings?" Old Bill's smirk widened.

"No, no."

Charlie's sentence rolled off of Old Bill's: "She has life insurance and he wants us to kill her!"

"Will you two shut up and listen for a minute?" Sticks cut their fun short. "I'm having a listen to whatever I can hear in the waiting room, as usual. Then this guy taps my shoulder.

Middle-aged. Good-looking chap."

Both Bill and Charlie looked at each other, trying to hold in their laughter.

"I didn't know you were that way inclined, Sticks?" Old Bill couldn't hold it in anymore.

His laughter ran around the interior of the small van, as his belly shook in every direction.

"Good skin, like. Well looked after, I mean." Sticks smiled as he shook his head.

"Looked like he'd had an easy life, ya know? None of those stress lines, or sun-scorched skin from working in the sun and the likes, like us lot. Anyway he tells me he works for The Badger."

Sticks continued to ramble on.

"He knows about a large sum of money."

The van stopped and Old Bill stopped laughing. It was as if Sticks had just informed them he had spit in one of their sandwiches at lunchtime, and they now had to guess which sandwich. Sticks became aware of both his friends' eyes gazing at him. Old Bill sat back in his seat.

"Now I'm listening."

"He wondered if I were the type who'd know the type, who would be willing to break a commandment? Ya know, the old *thou shalt not's*. Says he might know of a large amount of money being moved soon, and he wondered if I'd know a couple of guys who could 'forcefully' remove it from his possession, if they knew when and where."

"Oh yeah?" Old Bill interrupted. "Then why doesn't he get his own mates to mug him?"

"That's exactly what I asked, and he says because they'd be the first The Badger and the police, if he reported it, would go to. If the money went on the hop, like."

A rare silence filled the van. Sticks continued telling them about his waiting room encounter.

"He needs someone completely unconnected to him."

Sticks was interrupted again, this time by Charlie, in that teacher's voice.

"A stranger, someone from the doctor's waiting room." Charlie flipped the sun visor down and looked at the tiny photograph. "Are you mad? It's a wind-up or a setup. What are you talking about? Tell him, Bill."

Old Bill took some time before he spoke.

"Yeah well, if it was legit it would certainly help with a few of the bills, you know."

Charlie unintentionally appeared to be driving faster.

"What? You're supposed to have more sense! You're having a bad influence on him. I knew it was a bad move, letting him move in with you when Karen left you. You see what's happened?"

"Letting?" Old Bill shouted. "Letting him move in with me? The only reason why he's in with me is to help with rent. If Sticks wasn't helping me out I wouldn't be able...the house would be gone..." he struggled to keep his train of thought.

"Yeah, I know." Charlie's knuckles went white as he gripped the steering wheel tighter.

"I know. I know what they're like. I'm sick of it, sick of hearing it, sick of reading it.

What did we ever do to...? But that doesn't mean we can go through with what *he's* talking about."

"Don't argue, you two. I was just saying..." Sticks sat on his hands.

"How many have you missed?" Old Bill opened the glove box.

"Why not, Charlie? I mean, it's a criminal's money. It'd be like Robin Hood-type stuff."

Sticks fought his corner.

"I haven't missed any. Have you been reading my...?" Charlie reached across his friends and grabbed the bank's letter from the van hideaway.

"Yeah, but we wouldn't be giving it to the poor, would we? We'd be robbing it for ourselves. That would make it Robbing Hood!" Charlie shoved the envelope into the pocket of the driver's door.

"We are the poor, Charlie." Old Bill's deep voice silenced the cab. "It's ok to say, Charlie. You're trying and I get it, we're all trying. But I don't think we can win this one. Not when the people we're up against keep cheating and changing the rules whenever they want."

Charlie stopped the van outside the house Old Bill and Sticks now shared and closed his eyes.

"It's alright, mate. You're not on your own. We're not on our own. There are loads of people going through it, all different people." Bill twisted to sit sideways on the left side passenger seat.

"Yeah, man, one for all..." Sticks threw his arms around Charlie's limp body.

"How'd you know?" Charlie struggled to hold back some tears.

"I didn't read your mail. I didn't have to. Katie told me." Old Bill seemed to be coming accustomed to using his newly found soft tone of voice.

"I knew she would." Charlie opened his eyes, which let water run down his cheeks.

"It'll be alright, man."

Sticks pulled the sleeve of his sweatshirt up over his fist, then used it to wipe Charlie's face.

Chapter 3:

———

This is It

Charlie's face scrunched up as he ran the check list through his head, for what must have been the thousandth time.

"Everything had been organised," Sticks heard Charlie reassure himself with a whisper.

The three lifelong friends sat in their usual seats squashed inside the van's cab, waiting for the navy blue van. They were dressed head to toe in white disposable overalls. The trio looked as if they were moments away from inspecting a crime scene. On the contrary, if all went to plan they would be about to *create* a crime scene. Charlie's face relaxed, as he finished his mental list one last time.

Charlie sat in the driver's seat, gripping the steering wheel so tightly his knuckles turned white. Just as his grip was about to give in and loosen, he twisted at his wrists, as if trying to pull the wheel from the dashboard. Sticks looked as white as his overalls, so much so that you could not tell where his skin ended and the fabric began. Bill was sweating like an Olympic runner on his final lap. The window nearest Bill fogged up. Their breathing patterns were irregular, sometimes holding their breath with anticipation, until their lungs would notify them that they would have to remember to breathe again. The van sat parked on a small country lane.

A deep ditch ran each side of the road. It housed a collection of nettles, thorns and blackberries.

The road appeared wide enough for one and a half cars, completely impractical. They sat and waited.

"How long's it been?" Sticks shifted in his seat.

"45 minutes" Charlie whispered, without looking at any clock.

We've been set up. Charlie didn't dare frighten the lads by voicing his thoughts. *Any minute now the Gardai will pull up beside us.*

In that very moment a navy blue van appeared within sight. Charlie could see it approaching in his rearview mirror. It appeared to be only the size of his fist, from this distance, getting bigger and bigger on approach.

"This is it boys," Charlie notified his friends.

The three friends jumped out of the van and stood in against the ditch. The navy van paused in the middle of the little lane and slid open its side, just long enough for Charlie, Sticks and Bill to dive in. The van continued down the country lane, now with its new occupants inside. It was dark. Charlie could feel the bodyweight of Sticks lying across his legs and he was almost certain the soft padding beneath his head was Old Bill. It was silent, not a single sound apart from the squeak of the rear suspension as the van bounced over the old country road. Moon-like pot holes laced the lane. Charlie could slowly feel his eyes becoming accustomed to the darkness. He could just about see the inside of the door they had come through.

"Charlie?" A small voice called out in Sticks' tone.

"Shhh!" Charlie replied.

Suddenly they felt the van jolt forward and all three friends were involuntarily repositioned in seconds. They had stopped. They struggled to hear what had to be the driver and passenger door open, then slam shut again. The van lifted in height between the two door noises. The two voices from the driving cabin had disappeared.

Four and a half minutes. Charlie counted the seconds as they passed.

He could also hear each one tick by on Old Bill's watch, resting inches from his ear in his current position. The van lay so quietly that the ticking, accompanied by Charlie's heartbeat, sounded like a gong being beaten by a muscle-bound man. Then, after almost five minutes of silence, something happened.

'Sccchuuh.' A loud, metal-on-metal, sliding noise.

Was that really loud or have my ears just become accustomed to the silence? Charlie did not have the time to come to a conclusion.

A small hatch had opened on one side of the van's rear cabin. A beam of light shone through and painted a frame of light appeared on the opposite wall of the inner van. The sunlight instantly highlighted speckles of dust in the air.

'BANG!'

A large hard case was placed on the edge of the floor of the van, just inside the hatch, having been pushed through the small opening. It was pushed and slid along the floor by faceless hands from outside.

'BANG.'

Another case appeared in the opening, then two more cases followed.

'Sccccchuuh'

The hatch shut tight and the three friends found themselves feeling like prisoners, having just been freed. Charlie struggled to identify the murmur of voices as they walked up the side of the van.

"You go with him. Don't go down Santry Lane, stay on the M1. You're driving and I'll be behind ya, with these two."

"You're going with him?"

"Shut up and get in!"

"Yeah, it's just you don't usually come with us."

"And why the fuck would you care where I am? There's a lot of money in that van. My money! And I'm not about to take me fucking eyes off it until it's in a safe place. Right? Now,

I'm going in the car behind with him. Have you got a fucking problem with that?"

"No, no, I was just saying, like..."

Charlie knew the voice and he knew it well. The Badger had been involved in drug smuggling and dealing, armed robbery and kidnapping from a young age. He was well-known to the police and everyone who lived in the city of Dublin. Although Charlie had never been involved in any such activities, he knew the Badger well. Charlie had sat beside Michael Reilly for six years in Saint Catherine's primary school. Even then, Michael Reilly sported three randomly-placed white tufts of hair amongst his black. It was Charlie who had first told him he looked like a badger.

Charlie hadn't seen Michael since the last day of sixth class, aged thirteen. They each attended different secondary schools and had very different lives from that point onwards.

Charlie often wondered if The Badger would recognise him, if they were to ever meet again. He of course knew Reilly, given his presence in the paper every week. Charlie contemplated that reunion often. But not know.

The badger's voice had moved to the rear of the van. However, Charlie heard it get louder as he walked back up along the side of the van to the driver.

"Just saying, were you?"

"Ugh!"

Charlie heard the driver of the van wheezing in pain.

"Now, you won't be saying any more. Ah, you dirty bastard! I can't get me knife back out! You! Go with him in the van. You do something with this prick and I'll drive the car behind.

I liked that knife. But I'm still not taking me eyes off that fucking money. Get in! Let's get fucking moving, if we wanna be back for the match. "Charlie hoped his vantage point, close to the side door of the van, gifted him better audio of what just happened than Sticks and Old Bill. The last thing he needed was to spook them.

What have I gotten myself into? I should be at home with Katie. They can have me. I never wanted to bring this world anywhere near Katie.

Charlie regretted have ever contemplated meeting Michael The Badger Reilly again. The sound of the driver's door opening was getting familiar. This time it was accompanied by the downward shift of the van, having gained the weight of two front passengers.

Something feels different, Charlie worried. *What was it? That doesn't matter now; keep your mind on the job, Charlie.*

The van jerked forward. Charlie, Sticks and Old Bill stumbled towards the rear, but steadied themselves fast enough to not make too much noise. Old Bill wrinkled his forehead, then looked to Charlie. A moment passed as Charlie listened. Charlie skipped to back of the van.

As quickly as he could, whilst remaining silent, he removed the bulb used to light the registration plate of the navy blue Ford Transit. Once it was in his hand, he could use the slight gap it left to see what he could of Reilly behind.

Thanks be to God he didn't take the Audi. Charlie pushed the bulb back into place.

Sticks grabbed the case which had first come through the flap. He pulled it nearer to his feet.

Picking it up, he stumbled forward slightly. He readjusted his stance and tried a second time. He clutched it as if it contained a heart, ready to be transported into his own chest. Old Bill lifted another of the cases, the one which lay next to him.

Charlie walked past his case towards the rear of the van. Dropping to one knee, he 'proposed' to a handle on the floor. His knuckles turned a familiar shade of white as he grasped the lever on the floor hatch. He waited, and then the van stopped.

That's one, Charlie thought to himself, fighting the temptation to say it aloud and make such a fatal error. His inner desire to communicate made him involuntarily hold up his index finger on the other hand. He blatantly moved his lips and mouthed the words "That's one stop" and used his gesture to stress his point. Sticks got into position. He was now sitting on the floor with his heels against his bum. The case rested on the floor in front of him, between his spread knees. Sticks looked at Charlie and held the thumb of his right hand in the air. Old Bill stood behind Sticks, case in hand.

The van started to move again. Within the front cab sat two men. The driver looked food-deprived, he was so thin; he wore a white shirt that read 'You'll never beat the Irish' in slanted green letters. His clothing almost identically matched the passenger next to the window, save for the slogan. The second, much fatter man's T-shirt read 'Come on the boys' and was black. The driver's hair was black, short and parted to one side, and he wore rough stubble. The man next to the window sported a tightly cut head of red, wiry hair. By default and not by choice, he wore a large scar down his left cheek, a very noticeable landmark on his face.

Sticks remembered noticing it when he met him in the doctor's waiting room, some three months ago. The third man would appear familiar to everybody in the city. These two men were familiar to most residents of Dublin city and it surroundings. They regularly joined Michael Reilly as he displayed his personal photo album across the front pages of the evening newspapers. They, too, had grown up with a finger in every pie of the crime ring's banquet.

The Badger was a multi millionaire due to his personally-run theft, fraud, drugs and a blackmail racket. Reilly was only fifteen when he got into crime. His older brother and father before him had paved the way. Reilly had worked hard in his business in order to earn his place in line. Inevitably, he followed in the footsteps of seniors in the generation before him. His uncle had run the show for many years and, rumour had it, Michael's older brother, tired of waiting for his chance, did away with the uncle to gain superiority. It was not long afterwards that Michael, then aged just twenty-two, had started running the scene when his brother was reported missing.

The Badger sat in a black Humvee behind the packed van. The two stones of extra weight he carried did not help him regulate his body temperature. Luckily, the green nylon Republic of Ireland football jersey was not the type to show sweat patches. A bead of sweat ran down his forehead, as he lowered the driver's window and lit a cigarette. The temperature on that particular summer's day was over nineteen degrees. Inside the cab of the blue van was like a hothouse, the heat exaggerated through the windows. The two men showed signs of their Irish blood in such alien temperatures. Wet patches appeared on their shirts, under both arms and at the bottom of their lower backs. The cab was silent as they stopped at the traffic lights.

"That's two stops," Charlie mouthed in silence to Sticks. Charlie looked over Stick's head to Old Bill, who got into position, beginning to crunch down to a similar position as Sticks.

The van started off again. Charlie looked at Sticks, tilted his head and raised an eyebrow, desperately trying to convey "Are you ready?" to his friend without saying a word. Sticks looked over both his shoulders, a quick glance at his case, and finally at the handle within Charlie's grip and nodded. The van came to a stop for the third time. Bumper to bumper, the vehicles waited for the red light to change at the top of Capel Street. Charlie twisted the handle and pulled the hatch. It separated itself from the floor and, in fluid motion, Sticks stuck his legs through the new hole and dropped to the pavement beneath. He quickly rolled a couple of inches to one side as Old Bill's legs came through the hatch after him.

Fat old man, my arse, Charlie thought, as he smiled at Old Bill's agility.

Old Bill dropped down and out, rolling to the opposite side under the van. Charlie took his case and dropped it through the hole, then climbed through after it. He grabbed the lid of the hatch from within the van and pulled it across the hole in the floor.

'Schump'

It suddenly dropped into position, inches away from his face, where he now lay under the van.

The thin extra layer that the overalls provided did little to stop the cold ground's pinch. Sticks was to his left and Bill to his right.

"Don't you move, Sticks," Charlie calmed his thin friend. If only slightly.

Sticks' trust in Charlie was justified, as the van rolled forward and drove away down the street. The three friends were left horizontal in the middle of the road, like a man-made zebra crossing, the white overalls contrasting with the black of the tarmac. Sticks and Old Bill both jerked as if to get up. Charlie let go of the case resting on his chest momentarily, to grab the sleeve on the overalls of both his friends.

The massive black Humee drove straight over the top of the three friends. The next car almost did not see them, either. At the last minute the driver noticed the white of their overalls and jammed on the brakes. Charlie sat up. Raising one hand to the driver, Charlie mouthed his apologies in silence. He helped Old Bill to stand up as the horns of cars began to sound. Sticks quickly jumped and skipped onto the narrow footpath, briskly walking the opposite way back down Capel Street.

A short walk and a sharp right led the three into Parnell Street. Stopping at the corner, their unusual behaviour was beginning to attract glancing eyes. Quickly, they stripped off their white overalls to reveal three pairs of jeans and three bright green Republic of Ireland football jerseys. They walked briskly up the busy street towards the Woolshed bar. The seconds seemed like hours and the hours like minutes. Charlie heard the sports bar before he could see it.

Cheering, singing and chants of 'Come on you boys in green' sounded like angels to the three friends now.

The crowd of Irish fans were halfway through their celebrating and the game not yet begun. Charlie crossed the street with Sticks and Old Bill in tow. Crowds of similarly-dressed men and women, partaking in the random singing, filled the footpath outside the Woolshed sports bar.

Charlie did not waste a second. He removed the backpack from his back and held its handle tightly. Trying to keep the bag as close to his leg as possible, he crab-walked through the crowded bar. Reaching the raised opening in the counter, he placed a foot just inside the no-go area and leaned towards a young barista pulling a pint.

"Any chance you could look after a few bags in the back, just until the match is over?"

Charlie asked, inches from her ear, in order to be heard over the herd in the bar.

"I'm not really supposed to." The young girl stopped, halfway through pulling the pint.

"I just don't want to leave them on the floor for someone to fall over." Charlie finished this request with a handsome smile. By now Sticks and Bill had finally caught up with Charlie, having lost him in their meandering through the crowd.

"Yeah, go on, give them here." The young barista topped up the pint.

"Thank you. Really, I appreciate it..." Charlie beamed at the blonde barmaid "...you have no idea how much" he finished, under his breath. He kept the bag low and passed it through the opening.

"Thanks. There are only three of them and they're not too big."

"Are you going to let go of it or what?" the lady struggled to tug the bag from Charlie's hand.

"Yeah, yeah. Sorry"

His immediate reaction was to cling on for dear life. The realisation that he and the money would have to momentarily part ways had just set in.

"They'll be alright, won't they?"

"Ah yeah, there's a cloak room out the back. I'll throw them out there until you want them back."

The girl took the first bag and walk through the bar out of sight. Charlie felt a lump in his throat. Finally she returned. Sticks and Bill struggled to get the backpacks from their backs, edged in between the crowd. Then, like a game of pass the parcel, Bill handed his bag to Sticks as Sticks freed his hands, passing his bag to Charlie. Within seconds, both bags were in the barista's hands where she stood behind the bar. As she walked away, the three friends appeared frozen.

"WAIT!" Charlie shouted.

"What is it now?" The barmaid, half way up the inside of the bar, turned impatiently back to the trio. "Do you want them in the back or not?"

Bill and Sticks both remained in silence as they stared at Charlie.

"Yeah...Just stick us on three Guinness as well, would you? When you get a chance."

"Three Guinness? On the way." With the nod of her head the girl turned to stash the bags.

***

The navy blue Ford Transit was not even a year old. It was in near perfect condition. The black Humvee that Michael The Badger Reilly drove that day, was one possible out of a bunch. He owned cars, jeeps, motorcycles, quads, jet skis - you name it, he owned one. It was a haul that resulted from the simple equation: money plus stupidity multiplied by a desperate need for attention. As the Transit turned left into a cramped lane in the inner city, the Humvee followed.

They passed a six-foot square billboard which read:

24-Hour Mechanical and Crash Repairs.

Such a little car garage was not a rarity in Dublin's inner city, in fact the city was littered with them. Regularly run by men of a previous generation with more knowledge than hygiene. These are type of men who spent their youth on the streets of Dublin, with boys similar to Michael Reilly and his friends. The type of men who have seen the road ahead and taken the exit marked "honest hard work".

The Badger opened the rear door of the Transit before either passenger had the chance to open theirs.

"What time is it? I don't want to miss the start of the match..." Reilly rambled whilst throwing open both doors.

"Won't make it back of to my place. Might head into town to see it..." Reilly's face appeared red.

"Where's the bags? What's going on here?" Reilly's forehead pushed downwards. He slammed the back door of the Transit van. His hands outstretched, he turned towards the two men who had, by now, removed themselves from the vehicle. He grabbed the dark-haired man by the face and held it tight as he pushed him to the ground.

Where...is...the...money?" Reilly squeezed his fingers together.

Finally, Reilly let go his grip and, standing up, he straightened his T-shirt, as he made his way into the mechanic's garage at the top of the skinny lane way. Passing his red-haired friend, he stuck a finger into his cheek and pushed. Hard.

"Do you have anything to do with this?"

"No, adge...I...woo."

The red-haired young man had not foreseen such a situation when he had so casually approached Sticks in the doctor's waiting room.

"No, I woo woo woo! You stuttering fucker! No, you wouldn't have the bollocks to, would you!" The Badger walked into the garage, took a large can of petrol and returned. As calmly as a sloth, Reilly knelt on one knee beside his friend, who had worryingly remained frozen in the position Reilly had left him in.

"You!" Reilly looked at the red-haired man. "Hold this fucker down."

"No, no! Michael please, I didn't have anything to do with this. I promise. You were behind us the whole time. I have no clue where or how or - I promise. Please! No! Please?"

The outstretched man pleaded as he looked into the eyes, not of Michael Reilly, for there his pleas would have been wasted, but of the red-haired youth.

The regret of having ever planned this sleight of hand banged on the side of his skull, as the man held to the ground screamed. The man continued to scream until petrol filled his mouth, throat and lungs. Petrol overflowed back up and out of his nose and mouth, until the flow of petrol was the only movement he felt. Reilly removed his knee from the tarmac-covered ground and brushed it off.

"Do something with that. I'm going to see this match."

Reilly handed the empty petrol can to the young red-haired boy and got into his Humvee.

His hands felt greasy as he watched the black Humvee reverse out of the lane, without Reilly glancing back at him.

***

"I can't believe we did it!" Old Bill was already one pint ahead of his friends. "We managed to get our hands a hundred grand and we just walked away, and I have to tell you that I thought I'd feel guilty, because I was well brought up. But I don't feel guilty at all! We took that money from where it would have only been put to bad. Free like a regular Robin Hood and all that robbing from..." Old Bill raised his half-empty second pint high into the middle of the table.

"...The Badger!"

Sticks stared past Bill straight to the entrance of the pub.

"Yeah, well I was going with the rich. But if you're going to be specific, yeah. The Badger, and giving to the..."

Old Bill raised his glass again having lowered it momentarily.

"No! The Badger! Michael Reilly! There he is at the door!"

Sticks' eyes had not moved.

"Both of you keep your voices down. Stay calm and watch the match." Charlie walked away from the high table where his friends stood.

"Stay calm? He's after following us here! He's going to kill us or something!" Sticks quickly drank a mouthful.

43

Charlie walked back further into the crowded bar and stopped where opportunity allowed full sight of Reilly, without being noticeable. Charlie sipped at his frothy pint as he watched.

Reilly stood at the bar as he drank his first drink. The large screen demanded Reilly's eyes, helping Charlie to remain in the background. Charlie walked to the opposite end of the bar.

"Three more pints of Guinness." Charlie held three fingers aloft as he finished his order with a casual glance down the bar. He needed no more than two minutes of viewing Reilly's mannerisms before drawing a conclusion. He approached his friends, drinks in hand.

"He knows the money is gone. But I don't think he knows who took it," Charlie whispered into the ear of his skinny friend. "I don't know if your mate squealed on us, but if he does know we were involved, he definitely does not know we're in here."

Sticks' eyes widened around Charlie's eyes.

"Pot luck."

Charlie shrugged his shoulders.

"Luck..."

Sticks voice squeezed out of his lips like the air out of an unsecured balloon.

"Luck? Nothing lucky about it. Unlucky, I'd say. What are you talking about?"

Charlie smiled at Sticks and left him to his own demise, as Sticks rambled into an inaudible murmur. Bill finally opened his eyes and lifted his head. Charlie winked at his barrelling friend.

"As long as neither of you make us stand out in any way from this crowd, we'll be fine."

Chapter 4:

———∾∾———

This is Bad

"This is bad, this is so bad" Sticks protested, whilst holding the newspaper.

The three friends sat at the back of their old red van, outside yet another auction house. They were taking a well-deserved break, having just transported hundreds more priceless art pieces and furniture to their new temporary home at The Charlesmount Auction House.

Sticks sat on a scruffy upside-down bucket and, holding the newspaper open between his knees, looked worried, more worried than both Charlie and Old Bill had ever seen him. Possibly even more than that time when he was sent to the school principal's office, for accidentally smashing the large statue of Saint Patrick. The statue that had long stood intact in Saint Mary's National School. More nervous than that time he was caught by his mother with his dad's Playboy mags, at the age of thirteen.

"Charlie? What are we going to do?"

Charlie did not appear to answer quickly enough for Sticks' newly acquired impatience, as he quickly continued:

"Charlie, Michael Reilly! Michael fecking Reilly! Michael-hunts-you-down-and-kills you-Reilly! Michael-chops-your-nuts-off-and-feeds-them-to-you-Reilly! He never told me there was that much money!"

Charlie stood holding a cup that showed some signs that it used to be white. It now looked a light brown, stained from tea breaks that had come and gone. His forehead scrunched up.

"OK, we didn't know there was that much money when we set out to do this, but we knew what we were doing. And still we took it. We stole it, so we face the consequences."

Charlie paused and looked up from his cup. The swirling brown water had held his attention while giving his little morality speech, then he finished.

"When and where, Sticks?"

Sticks looked at up at Charlie, then he glanced at Bill sitting next to him, before finally looking back at Charlie.

"The quarry on Hillsdale Road. Tonight."

Chapter 5:

Just Us

Katie looked at Charlie. She really looked at him, not a passing look or a vacant stare, like we all use to show that we are aware of someone's presence. Katie looked into his eyes, as if God had told her they held the answers to the meaning of life. For her, they did hold the meaning of life. Charlie was her life, her one and her all, her everything. Her eyes moved across the mantelpiece to the next photograph. Had it really been that long? They looked like kids. They could not have been more that twelve or thirteen. Stood next to one another, Katie and Charlie filled the frame.

Another photo showed a larger group of young friends. Laughing and joking like nothing else mattered. Katie and Charlie once again stood next to each other, amongst the group. Katie and Charlie had always stood next to each other. Smiling to herself, she walked into the kitchen and sat at the table. From where she sat she could hear the van's brakes whistle, as Charlie brought it to a halt at the top of the driveway. She loved that sound. On hearing the familiar sound on this occasion her body became numb.

The air in her lungs crawled up into her throat, mixed with saliva and formed a ball, which lodged there and prevented her from swallowing. Moments had passed by the time she cleared the blockage and, by now, she could hear the key turn in the front door just down the hallway. The clanging of the key ring on Charlie's keys reassured her it was him.

"Hello." Charlie's voice came down the hall through to the kitchen. Katie stood up from the table and pushed the chair back across the kitchen floor.

'EEEeerrrth' the polished tiles screamed.

She immediately became aware of her surroundings once more. She was in their kitchen, Charlie and Katie's kitchen. The kitchen in the house they had bought together just after her twenty-fifth birthday. Had it really been two years ago? She had worried the house would be too cold with only the two of them living there.

"It won't be like my Mam's house," she protested for a short while. But she loved every room of it. She had always considered herself a naturally cold person anyway.

"Cold hands, warm heart." Katie whispered her mother's old saying to herself.

"Not too big, not too small, and enough room to have a few smaller guests at some time in the future." Katie quoted the words Charlie regularly used to describe the house.

The house was predominately white, save for its grey slate roof. There were bunches of beautiful flowers in window boxes under each of the windows to the front. Purples and yellows, reds and blues and whites and pinks ran up each side of the garden. All of these colours complimented the shining blue wooden front door. Standing proud, the door was fully aware it was the seal that had held many happy memories within the walls of this house. Katie had seen this house every time she closed her eyes since she was a little girl. She had described it to Charlie when they were teenagers.

He had struggled to make payments on the mortgage since the day his pen left his name on the agreement. Of course neither he nor Katie could find reason to care, he had her and she had him. Anything else seemed like an extra added bonus. If it were to be taken from them, then so be it. As long as they had each other. If something would threaten to take them from each other, now that would cause worry.

"Katie" Charlie's voice rang out again, this time much closer. "I've been calling you all the way up the hall. Why didn't you answer?"

The words had left his mouth before he had the chance to look at her properly. Seeing Katie's dazed face, Charlie considered asking again. He found himself questioning what Katie's body language had already made certain. Katie's voice crackled from the congestion in her throat. She had not spoken aloud for an hour or two.

"Doctor Lynn spoke with me earlier today" Katie eventually said.

Katie and Charlie had been trying for a baby for a year and a half, ever since they had settled into their new house. Charlie's mind could not find an emotion to paint onto his exterior.

Please God don't tell me we cannot build a family together. Please don't tell me the doctor pointed the blame at either one of, us.

"And…?" Charlie eventually plucked up the courage to ask.

Katie took a deep breath, then cleared her throat with a feeble yet appropriate cough.

"She didn't say we couldn't have babies. She explained we are compatible." Katie was smiling whilst her lower lip started to shake uncontrollably.

Charlie smiled back slightly confused.

"It just…she found something that we'll have to fix before we start trying again, that's all." Katie tried to compose herself in between her words.

Charlie smiled again. "That's great, we can build a family." *I can give her a family.*

Katie had not yet approached him. Charlie was certain news such as this should have ended in a loving embrace from his wife. Katie had more to say. She held herself stiff and looked him deep in the eye. He didn't say anything, just waited.

"She found cells, some bad cells." Katie stepped closer to Charlie. Charlie closed his eyes.

Cells! Please God let it be me. I'll take the blame. Just don't let it be her. I'll gladly take anything for her, any disease. I'll die for her. Do you hear me?

"They found cancerous cells, Charlie…" Katie rested her hand on Charlie's chest as he held her hips and pulled her closer. Katie wrapped her arms around his waist laid her head on his shoulder. Her usual immortal drive for cleanliness seemed to disappear now. Charlie was sweaty and his clothes were covered in layers of weeks of dirt, from many hard days' work. That didn't seem to matter to her in these circumstances. Isn't it funny what can seem important?

She took her head from his shoulder and looked into his eyes. He recognised that look, they had been practising it since they were six years old. Katie's lips parted and Charlie gazed down at them. He wanted them to say 'We're going to get you better.' He wanted her to say *he* was the one who was sick.

"We're going to keep you healthy. We can change your diet and I'm going to ask for more hours' work in the office, so you can take some time off. I'll get a second job in the evenings if that's what it takes." Katie took a breath. "You can give up work. You can sell the van, the extra money will help …" The sound of Katie's voice turned to a murmur.

It was not that Charlie had stopped listening, it was more that his thoughts began to shout louder and demand his primary attention.

It is me! Charlie's mind quietened and his vision cleared. Katie was looking at his face, from chin to forehead and back again.

"Why do you have a big silly smile on your face, sweetie?

"Sorry, Boo, I zoned out a little. I was just thinking of some stuff. I am just so happy that you are ok. I was so afraid you were going to tell me something was wrong with you. Whatever happens to me doesn't matter as long as you are ok." Charlie pulled her closer, having loosened his hold to speak.

"No, Charlie. It's not just about protecting me. I am not capable of being me without you here beside me. You are all I have ever known, you're built into my life, my mind. I need you to stay here with me. You have my back and I will always have yours. I need you." Charlie felt her back within the calm of his hands.

"I'll fight anything thrown at me...once I know you're in my corner."

Instantly that previous look of shock left her and she began to glow. A smile crept across Katie's face as she once again brought her head to rest on his shoulder. Her whole demeanour filled with reassurance. Katie could always tell when Charlie was lying. She knew when he was worried or scared, a talent developed from years of practice. In this instance she could tell he wasn't lying.

He wasn't scared, he was less worried than when he had first walked through the old blue door.

He said he'd fight it and she knew he meant it.

Chapter 6:

―∾―

What Now?

"I would have loved to have seen their faces. I know Reilly is as hard as nails and there is not much that knocks him back, and he'd kill me if he knew I was slightly involved in robbing his money..."

"But..." Old Bill interrupted Sticks loudly, desperately trying to prompt him to finish his sentence.

"But..." Sticks spat out before taking a breath to go again. "I'd have loved to have been there to see his face!"

Bill struggled to hold his lips together. He didn't like laughing. His belly would shake and wobble and remind him of how overweight he was. However, he couldn't fight it and figured now was the moment to let go. He surrendered to his silly conscience and began to laugh with his friend. It had a floodgate effect and laughter seeped from all his pores and orifices.

"I haven't laughed like that in a long time!" Bill confessed, amidst more laughter. "I can only laugh like that around you two!"

"Aw, Bill!" Katie proclaimed disappointment in him. His belly jiggling had caused a small storm in the tea cup he was holding. It splashed out over and the edge and spilled onto Katie's table cloth.

"You're cleaning that." Katie pointed at the table.

"Oh, the…" Sticks egged his friends to say it with him. "I mean…business…voice."

All three friends said at an identical speed and tone. Old Bill continued to laugh while apologising. Both Bill and Sticks where locked in uncontrollable laughter fits, picturing the Badger's face as he and the two drivers opened the rear doors of the empty van.

"I bet he ruined the seats of that lovely expensive jeep when he seen the back of that van – empty!" Sticks spat out, in between laughs.

"I nearly ruined the seat of my trousers when he walked into the Woolshed." Old Bill jiggled some more.

"What?" Sticks realised Charlie wasn't laughing.

Charlie stood with one leg crossed in front of the other, leaning against his kitchen counter. He was warming his hands on a freshly-made cup of tea. The cup's faded picture of Mickey Mouse peeked out from between his fingers. That cup had been a present from Charlie's sister when he was a child and he'd had it ever since. He had kept the cup in the belief that it held good luck. Charlie stood facing the table where Bill and Sticks sat drinking and, in Bill's case, spilling, tea.

Katie folded the table cloth, freshly sprinkled by Bill's excited hand. She was red in the face.

"I'm sick of having to clean up after you lot." Katie couldn't help herself from smiling.

She enthusiastically fired it into the washing machine, turned back to the table, wiped the remains of Bills spillage, threw a tea towel over one shoulder, started up the washing machine and proceeded towards the kettle.

"More tea?"

"Are you still looking after us, Missus?" Sticks elongated his words slightly.

"Just doing my bit in this pick n' mix of a family I was left with!" Katie smiled.

"Thanks, Missus, you're a grand auld one."

Bill and Sticks, both synchronised in tone and timing, thanked her and apologised. Katie placed an array of biscuits on a plate, lined up like soldiers in perfect formation. Colour-coordinated and filed according to size and sugar content, she placed the plate on the table with pride. Katie's attention to detail was of the highest standard, a personality trait she bore with pride since the age of four or maybe five years old. She had always taken pride in whatever she put her mind to. *If you're going to do something, it's worth doing it right.* Katie's mother had ingrained this motto in her daughter from early in her life. Furthermore, *if you're going to do something right, there is a right way of doing it.*

She lived by this motto, and had come accustomed to many strange cleaning routines as part of her every day. Most of her day ran like clockwork. Things had to be folded a certain way, placed a certain way, cleaned a certain way, cooked in a particular way and hung a certain way.

'Having' to do things the way she did annoyed her sometimes, however not having things done to her personal standards annoyed her more, so she continued about her routines. They annoyed even Charlie more again, but he had become accustomed to them, having known her for most of their lives. He loved her despite them and because of them. You could see that on Charlie's face.

She stood back from the plate with pride. Charlie looked at her and smiled. Sticks folded the morning newspaper and placed it on top of the laundry basket which sat on the kitchen floor beside him. Still smiling, he watched Katie grab the laundry basket, leave the kitchen and proceed upstairs.

"Folding to do. You lads behave yourselves while I'm gone" she shouted, already half way up the stairs. She closed the bedroom door and sat on the very edge of the soft bed. The fresh smell of clean sheets invited her to lie back. She resisted.

"What is it? What is it?" Katie filed through the newspaper. "What was so funny?"

She was fully aware that if she wished to know, Charlie would tell her every little detail, so she chose this option.

"Michael Reilly's missing money? Ha-ha! Good enough for him." Katie saw the tea stain on the opposite paper. "This is the page they had opened, alright." Resisting no more she threw her shoulders back onto the bed.

"Little feckers."

***

Back inside the kitchen, Charlie interrupted the laughter

"What time do we have to be there?"

"Four-thirty a.m." Sticks answered, with a serious tone in his voice and a contrasting tear of laughter in his eyes.

"Good, the sooner the better. I don't want that money in this house." Charlie was firm, without raising the volume of his voice.

"Yeah, yeah, I know. The sooner the better." Sticks shifted in his seat. "I promise you, I had no idea there was going to be that much money. I was told one hundred thousand. " He shifted again.

"Can we see it one more time before we move it, Charlie?"

"Yeah, now that would be a great idea. Let's spread it out right here, all over my kitchen table!" Charlie sarcastically waved his hands over the kitchen tabletop.

Sticks smiled.

"I'm not serious, you plank! What if Reilly found something belonging to us in the van?

Or what if your boy squealed on us?" Charlie had looked down the hall at the front door twice already.

"Yeah, sorry, never thought of that." Sticks' smile faded.

"Or what if the Gardai found something belonging to us? They're not bog boys anymore.

They have forensics departments and everything now, CSI style. CSI Dublin, what?" Charlie looked at Old Bill.

Old Bill raised his mug full of tea to his lips.

"And what do you think the Gardai are going to be doing examining the back of Michael Reilly's van? Do you really think that when he realised his money was gone, he just strolled down to the nearest Garda station and told them all about it?" Sticks' eyes darted from Charlie to Bill.

"No, you..." Charlie's voice got higher this time. "How do you think that would have gone? Excuse me, but loads of illegal drug money is gone. Could your forensics team please come and examine the back of the van it was in? Oh, and please pay no attention to any of the result showing any details of the - possibly hundreds of - people I've tortured, mutilated and probably killed in it!"

"Oh, yeah, I never thought of..." Sticks smiled at his mistake."But that's a good thing, isn't it? No Garda involved."

"It's good and bad in a way." Charlie took the empty cups from the table. "It's good because there are less people looking for the money - and for us. There's less forensics and professionals and that sort."

"Yeah, yeah, that's what I was thinking." Sticks rustled his blonde hair as he scratched his head. "How is it bad?"

Charlie placed the cups into the dishwasher and turn to face his friends once more.

"Because if Reilly knows, or ever finds out, that we were involved, and there are no Garda involved, he can do with us what his imagination allows."

Sticks rested his head on his hand. "And what are we going to do when we can't exactly tell the

Guards "excuse me, he's going to kill us because we stole a million euros belonging to him?""

Charlie folded the tea towel the way Katie had shown him.

"So no we're not seeing the money one more time. We've seen it enough as we were counting it. Besides, I still can't get the smell off my hands."

The laughter had truly faded.

Charlie flicked his left hand to see his watch. That turn of his hand was like a conductor's direction to his orchestra. Bill and Sticks rose to their feet.

"Eight o' clock, that's eight hours. Get yourself home, get a few hours sleep, do whatever else you need to do to be ready, and be back here for four a.m." Charlie's final words were like a gunshot to a sprinter.

It was the last word to be said. On the way up the hall to the front door, they each looked at one and other several times, yet didn't say a word. Once more the trio remained silent as they walked down the hallway in Charlie and Katie's house. An ever-so-slight nod of his head, with his lips clenched tight, was all Charlie did to say goodbye as his friends departed. Charlie closed his big blue door and then his eyes.

Chapter 7:

———❧———

Rendezvous

'Buuuzzzz!!...'

Charlie's eyes shot open, courtesy of the mixture of vibrations from his mobile phone and the fact that he had his eyes closed, yet had not slept. He momentarily lost his bearings and struggled to recall where he was. Then familiar random objects reassured and reminded him where he had spread himself out.

"Bloody couch is not comfortable at all." Charlie rolled to one side and stood in the blackness of his living room. "First night I ever spent on the couch." He looked down at where had just not slept.

I should have started a fake argument, just to have a reason for sleeping down here, for when she asks.

He had remained in his clothes to hasten his getaway. As slowly as he could, he moved towards the hall door. He bent down to put on his shoes, lined up beside Katie's in the hallway.

He finished tying his laces and straightened his back. He froze, staring at the inside of the big blue door. *This is it I'm going to walk out my front door and do... my front door...in my house, that I bought with the girl of my dreams.* Charlie rubbed his forehead with a flattened hand. *It feels like only yesterday that I lay eyes on her for the first time. Time seems to go so fast and I think it's getting quicker the older I get. Just let the next few hours pass as quickly and as smoothly as the last ten years.*

The freezing night air brushed Charlie's face. He reached his front gate and could see Sticks and Bill come up the road towards him. They jumped into the old work van, quiet as mice, trying desperately not to wake a soul. There was nobody living on Charlie's road who would know Michael Reilly, but any kind of attention would complicate things and was best avoided.

Sticks shimmied across the van's bench seat. Old Bill heaved his heavy girth up onto the seat and ever so gently they closed the door.

"If I start this every one of my neighbours will be awake in seconds" Charlie whispered.

"Yeah, there'll be hundreds of little heads poking out the side of the curtains!" Sticks smiled.

"That's what you get for living in an old folks' village." Old Bill laughed then looked at Sticks to provoke him.

"It's not an old folks' village. I told you before there just happens to be a lot of elderly people living in this cul-de-sac." Charlie released the hand brake with the intention of rolling the van to the end of the street.

Right on queue, Sticks giggled to Bill. The bulky van creaked forward ever so slightly then refused to roll any further. Unconsciously, they each reacted to the situation in the same way. The three all rocked forwards and backwards in their seats, trying to shunt the van on with their hips. Like young children trying to start a swing. Realising the reflexive gyrating action they had performed, all three began to smile. They squeezed their lips together to prevent their laughter escaping on sleeping ears. Thankfully their hip-swinging had worked and the van slowly began rolling towards the end of the road. The van had just reached a safe distance when the laughter squeezed its way through Stick's lips. Old Bill quickly followed suit. Charlie joined the laughter as he started the engine in tears. They dwindled to a giggle as he pointed the van in the direction of the old quarry. The van crept across the sandy surface, raising a brown cloud which made the trio feel even warier of the situation. Charlie could see Reilly's man waiting.

"He's here early."

Charlie felt uncomfortable, for more reasons than the obvious ones. He had a great eye for detail, which he regularly used to notice small things about people when he met them. It was an unconscious thing at this stage in his life. His unease in this situation was increased by the fact that he had refrained from doing so, in the case of this guy. Charlie wanted to be able to drop him from his memory, as soon as this all came to a conclusion. He kept everything about him in an area of his short term memory, at a safe distance from where he kept the house, Katie, his Mum, Dad and the likes. Charlie brought the van to a halt.

"What's his name again?"

Charlie looked across the seat to Sticks and Bill.

"Steven." Sticks answered.

"Yeah, looks like a Steven. Right, this is it. You ready? Bit of luck he hasn't squealed and Reilly isn't about to pull in behind us." Charlie blessed himself, quickly tilted the sun visor down then back up quickly, before opening the door of the van. Old Bill, realizing his door had only been half-closed due to how lightly he had shut it, exited the van. Sticks poured out behind his friend. They walked towards the silhouette ahead of them. Steven stood in front of a car whose head lights beamed brightly.

Thirteen steps Charlie's head told him as they came to a stop. He remained unsure if he had counted out of habit, to settle his nerves, or to be a step ahead if a quick escape was necessary. The shadowed man was now close enough for some aspects of his face to be visible.

That would do nicely. If I couldn't see your face, you can't see mine.

Charlie knew Steven's face well enough from the papers. He did not need to get any closer.

"Empty hands, Paul" the shadow spoke with his gravelly tone.

Who the fuck are you calling Paul? First names now? I haven't called Sticks by his birth name in my life. Who does this guy think he's getting friendly with?

Years of referring to him by an assortment of nicknames almost completely erased the name Paul.

"You must be keeping well. I haven't seen you back in the doctor's office" the gravelly voice finished.

"Yeah." Sticks answered, then stopped to clear his throat, the dust reminding him that these were the first words he had spoken since exiting the van. "I've not been bad."

"Yeah, listen…" Charlie slid one foot round, drawing circles in the sand. "We haven't got a lot of time. None of us want to be out here longer than we have to be. You know being found in a quarry with three bags full of money, matching exactly the amount stolen in a recent robbery, is not the easiest of situations to talk our way out of."

Not impossible but certainly not easy.

"He's right" Steven's shadowed figure agreed.

"So, give me my three hundred thousand and be on your way."

"On our way" Charlie shifted weight from one foot to the next as he spoke. "Hold your horses." Charlie fought the urge to walk toward Steven.

"You knew how much was really in the bags?"

"Yeah, of course. I just knew you wouldn't go along with it unless it was petty cash."

Steven held both his hands stuffed into the front pockets of his tracksuit jacket as he spoke.

"There's just one problem with that. You see, we agreed your cut was thirty thousand and we think that's all you should get." Charlie pushed his chin up into the cold night air.

Sticks took one step to his left before he spoke: "Charlie, what are you doing?"

"Ha ha! No, no, my cut's bigger because your take-home is bigger. Nice try, though.

You see you have no idea what I've had to do to get that money. You've no idea what he's done...what he told me to do...Look, just stop fucking about and give me my cut."

Steven's left hand came out of his jacket pocket for the first time, as it nervously brushed his hair down flat. Charlie turned to Sticks.

"It's alright. If he had Reilly waiting nearby, he'd have given the signal already. You keep an eye on his right hand. If it comes out of that pocket, get back behind the van...and keep yours in your pocket, like you're holding something."

"Yeah, so there's another problem." Charlie raised his voice this time.

"You got a problem with more money?" Steven's shadowy figure replied, losing its calm demeanour.

Cracked him...his composure is gone.

"No, no problem with money. Just don't like suddenly having to hide three times the amount I had planned. We can't spend this money." Charlie squinted to see how the shadowy man would react.

"I like you, you have balls. You'd have to have balls to have agreed to this from the start." Steven calmed again.

"What do you mean we can't spend it? What else do you do with money?"

"Listen, I don't know about you but we're all working-class boys. We can't be seen to have come into such good fortune, so suddenly after a local robbery. The guards will have too many questions and if word gets out, Reilly won't have any questions - he'll just act." Charlie pictured the house being fully paid for. "So, the way I see it, we have to get this money offside until all this blows over." *Katie would kill me if she knew what I'm up to.*

"Yeah..." Steven rubbed his face with his palm.

"...That's pretty smart...when you put it like that...we don't have much of a choice. So, smart arse, what exactly do we do with it?"

"There's only thing we can do." Charlie looked every man in the eye. Struggling to see in the poor light, they each inspected the men next to them. Charlie took a dusty breath.

"We bury it. This place hasn't been open for about ten years. No one comes in here anymore, and they're not exactly going to start building here anytime soon, now that the building game has dried up."

"Here? What, like - now?" Steven pushed his toe into the loose gravelled ground.

"Have you got somewhere better to be?" Charlie finally allowed himself to take that step.

"No time like the present."

"Yeah, well what exactly are we going to dig with?"

Steven pocketed his loose left hand once more. Charlie looked at Sticks. Sticks proceeded to the back of the van.

Steven heard the rear doors close before Sticks returned, with four six-foot shovels. He walked into the middle of where all four men stood and dropped the tools in the sand.

"Right! Better to get it over with, then. Just let me throw this in the car."

Steven finally took his right hand from his jacket pocket. A weighted object, still inside, visibly protruded.

"What did you throw into the car?" Charlie stood on his toes.

"Ah, just in case you boys were acting the maggot or planning to do a burner with my cut. It's alright, though, you seem sound. I'll throw it in the glove box."

Steven's legs were all Charlie could see as the rest of him vanished into his vehicle. He quickly finished his business inside the car and returned to the centre circle.

"Ok, where do we start?"

"Right here."

Charlie handed him one of the shovels.

Chapter 8:

———∿∿———

Grave Digging

"Jesus Christ, I'm glad I do what I do to get money! All this working is a pain in the arse." Steven held his back as the three friends threw the last shovelfuls onto the fresh grave.

"Jesus, are yous not in bits?"

"No" Sticks laughed. "We're used to it."

Charlie used the back of his shovel to smooth the grave over.

"I'm glad you do what you do too, because you can't dig worth a shite." Even in the freezing night air, Old Bill was now covered in sweat.

"What?" Steven walked back towards his car.

"Spent half the night on a break and if you weren't on a smoke break you were pissing and moaning." Old Bill was mumbling, with his tired head resting its chin on his chest.

"Here, how long we talking?" Steven shouted from the car. "Leaving it here, like."

"We don't know." Sticks collected the shovels from Charlie and Bill.

"You don't know? This is your plan? Not a very good one if it's only really half a plan."

Steven walked back to the friends with another cigarette lit.

"I don't know." Charlie confidently announced. "And neither do you, or any of us, for that matter. So, for now we bury it. We walk away until the heat cools off a little, we see how this chooses to play out, and we agree to come back together when it is safe to do so. Until then, we're not seen together. Just in case any descriptions have put a red light on a similar group."

Steven laid the cigarette onto his lip and shoved his hands back into those front pockets.

"Here, how I know that you won't just come back out here tomorrow, or the next day, or whatever, and dig it and do a legger?"

"Because why bother coming out here and digging this hole? We had the money. If we wanted to cut you out, we would have done a runner without wasting our time digging holes, as fun as this has been and all." Charlie couldn't help himself watching that right hand, even though Steven seemed to have mellowed. Lowering his cigarette to speak, Steven did so whilst blowing smoke. "Here, how do you know I won't just come back out and dig it up?"

Old Bill took a quick step towards the youth. Sticks briskly wrapped his arm over Bill's shoulder and restrained him. Steven smiled and sat against his car's bonnet.

"Because, you're not very smart. Because if you do, I guarantee within days you will do something, or buy something, that draws attention and Reilly will know you were involved."

Charlie took the keys from his pocket and turned towards the van. The smile slid off Steven's face.

"You're a lot like him, you know. You remind me of him. Where are you from?" Steven raised his voice as Charlie increased the distance between them. Charlie opened the door of the van.

"Sticks has a contact for you."

Sticks turned to Old Bill and walked him towards the van as Bill proceeded to mumble. Charlie turned the van in a wide circle, thanks to the space the quarry provided. In the mirror mounted on the driver door he watch Steven step on his cigarette, then get smaller and smaller.

"Thank God that's done." Sticks held the bridge of his nose.

"God had nothing to do with it." Old Bill's T-shirt had a sweaty V-shape down the front.

Charlie lowered the sun visor, blessed himself then pushed it back up against the van ceiling.

"It's not done. It's only half done. The rest - the important part - is keeping our mouths shut and hoping that little fucker keeps his mouth shut, too...ouch!" Charlie grabbed the side of his head and winced. He let go of the steering wheel and began coughing. The van swerved across the empty road.

"Charlie! Are you alright, Charlie?" Sticks grabbed the side of the wheel closest to him and pulled it back to him, helping the van narrowly avoid the street light on the wrong side of the road. Charlie coughed and coughed. Bill tried to reach across Sticks to Charlie. Sticks grabbed the handbrake and pulled on it with everything his digging hands had left. Charlie spat blood as the van stopped diagonally across the street, one wheel up on the curb.

"Jesus, Charlie, are you ok?" Bill leapt out of the van and circled to the driver's door.

Charlie slid out of the van as Bill opened the driver's door. Between Bill and the driver's seat behind him, Charlie found a balanced stance.

"Yeah, yeah, I think so. Just lost my breath for a minute there." Charlie touched the centre of Bill's chest, still warm.

"Charlie, your hands are freezing. Come on." Old Bill placed Charlie's arm across his big, sweaty shoulders. "I'll drive us home."

Bill felt Charlie's limp frame unable to hold any weight as he carried his friend around the van to the passenger door.

"I'm ok. I'll be ok..." Charlie eyes were closed as he protested.

"Yeah, we know you will, buddy. I'll just drive to be sure. Give you a break for once.

Keep an eye on him."

The sound of the metal passenger door echoed up and down the empty early morning streets. Bill briskly moved around the van once more.

"Let's get us home." He turned the key in the ignition.

Sticks' face looked even more paler usual as he nodded his head under Bill watchful glance.

Chapter 9:

No News is Good News

Doctor Lynne's office was so quiet that Charlie was sure he could hear his blood pump through his veins. Katie was not making a sound next to him. She was no more than a foot away on Charlie's left. They both sat facing Doctor Lynne's desk, attentively examining its contents. The desk's contents consisted of an array of mundane items. Paperwork scattered about left and right, a photo frame, presumably containing a proud photo of the doctor's perfect family. The frame faced the window behind the desk so the photo was not visible from where the couple sat. Also on the busy desk was a computer, a monitor and a keyboard, a desk-tidy holding one pen and a model of some part of human anatomy.

That thing still looks like a sci-fi collector's prized possession. Who has a desk-tidy for only one pen? Oh come on, where are you Doctor Lynne? She's always late for my appointment.

In fairness, she's probably very busy in this place, but three years and never once on time?

Charlie scratched his bald head. He struggled to find the strength to extend his arm. He flicked his sleeve back.

"What time have you got?"

Katie smiled without showing her teeth. Charlie smiled back. Katie quickly searched through her bag and removed a hanky.

"Careful, Charlie, it's that side. Do you want me to get it?" Katie leaned over towards her husband with the hanky in hand.

"Oh thanks, Kay. No I can get it, sorry about that." Charlie's gums bled regularly.

"Still apologising?" Katie handed the hanky over.

The door behind them opened. It closed just as quickly. A doctor entered, along with a cool wind in the interval. Katie popped up to a standing position. Charlie slowly stood.

"Hello, Mister and Mrs Leary." The doctor flicked pages on a clip board and did not raise her eyes from the documents.

"How are you today? I hope you're keeping well." She held her hand out to the couple.

They each took turns shaking it. She finally raised her eyes from the paperwork.

"Yes, Doctor, thank you." Katie returned the smile.

Charlie remained silent. He held the tissue to his mouth.

"You have some more bleeding, Charlie. Are you ok? Would you like me to have a look?" The doctor circled the couple en route to her chair.

Charlie examined the doctor's tired face with inquisitive eyes. "No, its just the normal amount, thank you, doctor."

"Ok. I might arrange to have one of the nurses have a look at your gums when we finish here. It should not take longer than a few moments." Doctor Lynne smiled from behind her desk.

"Now, for today. Firstly, do either of you have any questions you would like to ask me today before I begin?" She sat.

"No, Doctor. We would just like to hear any news you might have for us. Everything is pretty much the same. Charlie is still struggling with energy, like me mentioned in our last visit."

Katie smiled. Charlie's eyes asked a million questions.

"Questions, no. I can't think of anything."

"What I have to tell you today is not easy." The doctor thumbed the pages continuously.

I'm sorry but could you be a little bit more vague, please doctor? What the fuck does 'not easy' mean? Katie quickly verbalized Charlie's thoughts, thankfully in a more mannerly fashion.

"Sorry doctor, could you be a bit more specific?"

"Of course, yes. I just wish to take some time so that we do not end up jumping to conclusions." The page turning finally stopped.

Her voice seems so serious. Much more serious than any of the last times. In all the years

I have had this, she's never sounded like that.

"You've been battling this for a very long time, Charlie."

Doctor Lynne started in her newly acquired tone. "As you know, we've tried many procedures to try to slow it down.

However, that is all we have been able to do, merely slow the process down. The treatments were always.....you understand...going to come..."

To an end. Charlie didn't flinch.

".....to an inevitable conclusion" As the doctor stumbled to a conclusion her shoulder slumped.

"There are no more treatments?" Katie reached across and held Charlie's hand.

"At this moment in time we have tried all the possible treatment available to us." It was almost like a whisper yet it rang loudly in Katie's head.

"At this moment in time...but they're always developing new treatments, right? The scientists are." Katie's eyes filled with tears. "We can just hang on in there and wait until a new treatment comes along, right?" Katie squeezed Charlie's hand.

Charlie usually whimpered when any slight form of matter touched his skin.

"A better treatment...?" She squeezed. Yet Charlie remained silent.

Chapter 10:

___

One Night

As Charlie and Katie arrived back to their perfect little home, the rain pelted off the car roof.

I don't think we've ever come back from Doctor Lynne's office so fast. I wonder will all time move this fast now? It seems different when you don't have as much of it.

Katie dropped her soaking wet handbag on the chair just inside the hall door. She removed her drenched coat as she followed Charlie to the sitting room.

"I can't lay on the bed with this thing." Charlie wrestled to remove an arm from his coat.

"You don't worry about that, just get yourself onto the bed."

Katie flung her long coat at the coat hook and helped Charlie with his. He stumbled like a zombie, within his own world. They had spoken very few words since Doctor Lynne told them the 'news'. Charlie reached the rug in the centre of the small sitting room. Soaking wet, he turned to face her. His lip shook uncontrollably as tears poured down his cold face. His voice, hoarse from under use, cracked

"Six months?"

Katie walked towards him with tears in her eyes to rival his. She placed her index finger on his bottom lip. It quietened his words and stopped the shaking. She then kissed it so to seal it tight. She broke from the kiss.

"I have always loved you...and forever."

Charlie held her in his arms. He began to lose his balance, yet did not want to let go, a battle Charlie was clearly going to lose as he, with Katie in his arms, began to sway. Still he refused to let go of her and they stumbled to the rug. Katie and Charlie's laughter soon led to a similar kiss as before. That kiss led to another, and another, and on from there. This marathon of kisses quickened with pace and passion as they began to remove their soaked clothing.

"No matter what happens, I love you" Katie whispered.

Rain threatened to break the window panes of their little dream home. Katie leaned back and lit the six fancy candles she kept in the spotless fireplace.

"I love you, too."

Chapter 11:

The Test

Katie stood in the bathroom. The left side of her head was inches away from the mirror as she held her parted hair.

"Another grey one. I thought you weren't supposed to get these until you where much older than me." Katie spoke into the phone held to her other ear. "He's ok. He has gotten weaker again, further since Doctor Lynne's news. I'm telling you, Mam, it's only been a week and I can already see it. It has affected him." She pulled out the hair. "He doesn't talk as much...he tells me things but he doesn't always have the energy."

She sat on the edge of the bed. She could hear the clock on the locker ticking away.

"I've been struggling to understand. We have routines that we stick to, for Charlie, and they have been helpful for him resting and that...but then he deteriorates, and I just feel like I have been pulled in a different direction."

A mumble sounded from the phone.

"No, Mam, I don't want to think about anything else. Anyone else. Right now it's important that I think only about Charlie." Katie felt dizzy. "I'm thinking about him now. It's the only thing that makes me happy. I try to focus on him. It's better that constantly thinking about appointments, tablets, washing cream, bleeding and and and...sometimes I think so much I give myself a headache.

"Mam, I'm going to go. I have a bit of a cramp and besides, Charlie usually wakes around now, so I need to go check on him." The cramps continued. "Ok, bye, Mam. Bye."

Katie stood up from the bed. Immediately she ran back into the en-suite in which she had just checked her greys. The lid on the toilet would not open quickly enough as she gagged.

Finally it fell back against the cistern and she vomited into the bowl. For the first time in weeks she questioned how *she* was feeling. For the first time in a long time she thought of herself.

Her body felt broken and her mind continued to tie knots around Charlie. She struggled to raise her hand to flush the toilet, her brow beaded with sweat. She wiped her mouth with the back of her hand then somehow found the energy to push her body's weight up from the bathroom floor.

She walked in a zigzag from the bathroom to the bedroom, catching sight of herself in the mirror.

"What am I like?" The fright broke her train of thought and Charlie slipped from her mind. "What am I like?" Katie questioned herself.

Charlie lay sleeping in the sitting room. Once his health had deteriorated, Old Bill had dragged the spare bed into

81

the front room for handiness. Nobody else was home. Katie struggled to remember anything. Weeks - months - had passed by, and she was certain she must have done so, yet she could not remember washing herself, dressing herself or feeding herself. She had spent every day since visiting Doctor Lynne's thinking and caring for Charlie. She felt lost.

Suddenly a thought entered her head. She had no recollection of any bodily functions taking place in the months gone.

"When was the last time I..?" she continued to talk to herself. "Was I late...or early, maybe? When was it?"Her panicked voice was getting louder. "Could I be...pregn.?"

The thought ran fully through her mind, yet only half the words had the chance to escape. She was off, out of the bedroom. She snatched the dressing gown from the back of the door on her way past and she took the stairs two at a time. She leaped the last four steps and landed within reach of Charlie's spare work boots, which sat permanently by the front door. Slowing down for a second, she bent the handle of the door, to gently check on Charlie.

"Still sleeping like a..." She looked down at her stomach between the two lapels of the dressing gown. Quickly and as quietly as she could, she returned the door and released the handle. She pushed her feet into the damp boots and quickly proceeded towards the car. The engine started and the car left the driveway like a Formula One vehicle exiting the pits. She took a left at the top of the cul-de-sac in hot pursuit of the nearest shop, pharmacist anything that sold pregnancy tests.

Chapter 12:

Bundle of News

Charlie's eyes opened. *My back is killing me.* It had become increasingly more and more difficult to lift his own bodyweight without help. Even small movements such as changing sleeping position required at least one other person. Lying flat on his back, Charlie tingled with pins and needles from his head to his heels. He knew that six square feet of the ceiling of his sitting room better than anyone. He had seen this square more often that he had seen his own face in the past months. He had seen his own face more often than he had seen several of his old friends. A dullness hung in the air. The window on Charlie's right did not light the room the way it usually did in the mornings. The house seemed different.

"What is that smell?" Charlie raised his head from the pillow. *Turkey? Is that turkey? Oh, I can smell stuffing, too.* His head dropped back down. Just as these aromas had filled his entire body through his nostrils, he sensed a wave of warmth down his left side. The fire was lighting in the sitting room and the heat crept past Charlie and out the door, slightly ajar.

"What time is it?" *How long have I been asleep?*

Charlie's eyes were the only part of him that he could move without any pain. He squinted at the clock over the fireplace. *Five o'clock! How the hell did I sleep that long? Why didn't Katie wake me? Did I miss my medication? Where is Katie?*

"KATIE!" Charlie croaked out. *Oh God, I hope nothing has happened to her. I hope she's ok.* "KAY!" *What if she's fallen or hurt? Will I be able to get to her?*

He dragged his left leg the four aching inches it lay from the edge of the bed and allowed it to fall. His face visibly tightened. *Here we go. This one's got to go further. You can do this.*

His right leg took two efforts to get to the edge. Once there he slid it off the side and allowed the momentum of the drop sling his top half round and up into a sitting position. *Aaarrrgggghhhh!*

Charlie's arms sat limp by his sides, his hands lifeless on the bed. *Half way there. Here we go.* His stomach muscles cramped like he'd been kicked. His legs shook as they started to take his weight for the first time in a long time. *Shit, that hurts.* But he was up, standing on his own for the first the time in months.

"Ha ha, look at me...Katie!" He slid one foot along the floor in the direction of the door.

The next foot followed like a long distance skier. He shuffled, hold his aching stomach muscles.

"...Still crazy after all these years. We're still crazy..." *Paul Simon...What's going on?*

He pushed the sitting room door and it swung to prove his senses correct. The fire flickered in the sitting room and cocooned the room with heat. Charlie proceeded on into the kitchen. He stumbled in whilst the radio played and instantly found his eyes drawn to Katie. She sang quietly away to herself as she peered into the oven to check what looked like a beautiful turkey dinner. His eyes began to wander round the room. Two wine glasses, two plates, the good knives and forks and four candles sat, like small bedposts, in the centre of the table display.

"Dinner smells amazing" Charlie whispered. *Have I forgotten something?* An imaginary calendar appeared in Charlie's head. *No.*

"Oh my God! What are you doing up on your own?" Katie leapt over to Charlie and held him up by the waist.

"I called. I thought you needed me." An almost lifeless arm was slung around Katie's shoulder.

Katie walked him to the table and sat him at the top seat.

"I do need ya." She hunkered down beside him and briskly kissed the back of his feeble hand. Then she sprang up and bounded to the fridge. She grabbed a bottle of wine and quickly returned to his side.

"Are you ok?" Katie smiled.

"I am, yeah. A little sore but are you...ok? I mean?"

"Yes. Sorry, I didn't hear you call, sweetheart." Katie filled his glass. "I know this has been hard lately, and I can't begin to try to know how you're feeling, with all the news that has accumulated over the past few months. Well, sweetheart! We have more news!" She hunkered down beside where Charlie sat.

What? Charlie's eyes widened as he leaned back against the chair.

"Really? What is it?" *I don't know if I can take anymore...news. By news, does she mean good news or bad news?*

"But this time, it's good news." Katie added with a smile on her face. She held his gaze with her smile and told him with her eyes long before she ever opened her mouth to speak. Her hand slipped to rub her stomach.

"Sweetheart, I'm pregnant. We're pregnant."

"What?" Charlie spat out a mouthful of wine with surprise and excitement.

"How? When?" Each of his words got louder.

"How long? Wait! Is it mine?"

Katie laughed. "Of course it's yours, you cheeky oaf! It would hardly be good news if it wasn't yours, and besides...of course it's yours! What are you suggesting?"

Charlie threw his brittle body onto her, crouched beside him, and embraced her in his arms.

"Remember that night we came home from the hospital?" Her words were dampened by his shoulder against her mouth. The thoughts of that night made them both smile. They momentarily broke from their hold to look in each other's eyes. Charlie took some time to stand.

He then proceeded to shimmy towards the door.

"Where are you going?" Katie followed him across the floor.

"No, don't follow me. I'll be ok, I promise. I just have to do something. Stay there."

Charlie instructed with the confidence of his younger self. Katie sat at the table, filled her glass with water while refilling Charlie's with wine.

"EVERYTHING OK?" She shouted, unsure of how far he'd gone.

"I've had this a long time now." Charlie's voice was low as he came back round the door sooner than expected. "But when we got the news of my sickness, I felt it wasn't fair to ask you to commit to someone who wasn't going to be sticking around."

Katie's face crinkled up with disapproval at such a thought, however excitement quickly brought a smile to her face again..

"I want you to know this doesn't mean that you have to live your life alone when I'm...no longer around." Charlie continued.

"Don't talk like that" she quipped

But Charlie persisted. "We'd never have time to plan a wedding, never mind actually attend one, but all I ask of you is to remember me. Accept this..." Charlie could have fallen to his knees easily, however it took much effort to get into such a position slowly, without hurting himself.

Katie helped by holding his hands.

"What are you doing? Where are you going?"

"I'm kneeling, Katie. Will you accept this ring as a way of promising me you'll remember me?"

Tears filled up in Katie's eyes. She struggled to clear the lump in her throat. She eventually managed to swallow.

"Yes. Of course I'll marry you. I love you, I have always loved you and I promise I always will. It doesn't matter if we never get to have a wedding or a registered thing. In my heart and yours we are now married. I never have wanted, and I never will want, anyone else."

Charlie placed his ear to her stomach and hugged her around her hips. Katie hugged his head and they both began to laugh. Neither knew why. Perhaps all that sadness had built up over time, and now their bodies needed to wash it all away. It seemed this moment of joy had burst the floodgate and now happiness was washing them clean. Charlie held both Katie's hands in his and whispered in her ear

"If it's a girl, can we call her Jennifer?"

Jennifer was Charlie's mother and his grandmother before her. They where two women who Charlie felt he owed his life to. Katie knew the name held resonance with a very strong female presence throughout Charlie's life. Now he wished to continue that cycle. Katie smiled amid the laughs.

"If it's a boy, I'll still name him Jennifer."

Their laughter continued as they held each other. There was no happy ending, but right now this moment of happiness, of laughter and joy was all that mattered.

Chapter 13:

Reality Hits

Katie became aware of the cool wind blowing across the back of her neck. It felt insignificant to her now, she could identify it was cold. However she failed to feel her usual agitation towards it.

It was as if numbness had taken over her entire body. She lacked feelings of any sort, emotional or physical. That cool wind ravaged her hair around in front of her face. All eyes seemed to be examining her, over seventy pairs of eyes looking her up and down. The large turnout was due to Charlie's kindness and popularity. They had all arrived in grief, to say their goodbyes.

Katie stood between Sticks and Bill, holding her newly-arrived bump. Charlie's large traditional Irish family stood to Katie's immediate left. Sticks had never seen so many dry eyes at a funeral before. The cause of which was by no means a lack of sorrow, but a sense of awareness. This was something they had all been prepared for since Charlie's diagnosis. It appeared as if all tears had been shed in the months prior to this day. Charlie's family, friends and associates had all had time to come to terms with Charlie's inevitable end.

"I was only telling him last week how much of an impact he's had on the boys down the football club since his donation."

"Charlie was a true influencer."

"There really was nobody like him."

"He lived in this city all his life and the community will not be the same without him."

Words, words, words. Everybody had words to say. A flurry of random people approached Katie. She knew many of them very well. Some she recognised yet could not place.

Some, she was certain, she had never seen before. Some shook her hand. Some tried to touch her bump. She didn't like those. Indeed she liked some, disliked others, but none of it really mannered at all.

"I knew Charlie all his life..."

Katie was aware that no words could compare to Charlie, however she was pleased with the words Father Reilly had chosen to send her husband off. The words where pleasant and it seemed appropriate that Father Reilly deliver them. As tradition had it, Charlie's father removed his jacket as the blessing ended. Gerry rolled up his the cuffs of his shirt and took the shovel from an outstretched arm. He stood on the back of the shovel head once, and raised the dirt hidden beneath the surface. His 65 years struggled to lift the weight of the small shovelful.

Holding the soil over his son's coffin, he let the first soil fall onto his son's resting place. Gerry's brothers, each similar-aged, followed suit. As jackets were removed, shirt sleeves were rolled up and Charlie's uncles took turns shovelling the loose soil into Charlie's new bed. Each man passed the shovel to the next, each letting one small shovelful of soil fall. As Charlie's youngest uncle let the soil meet with the coffin, he turned and proudly held the shovel in his outstretched arm and into Old Bill's direct line of sight. Bill firmly took the shovel and added his dirt before holding the tool to Sticks' chest.

***

Sticks heard an imaginary bolt of lightning within his head. Momentarily blinded, he lost sight of where he now stood. He was transported back to that night, the night he, Bill, Charlie and Steven buried those cases. That night was cold, as was this very day at the graveside. The shovel looked identical to the ones they used that night and felt the same in his hand. Sticks remembered how uneasy he felt that night, irritated with heightened awareness. Filled with fear and worry in case they might have been seen. All his memories recalled bad feelings and emotions. However, he found himself wishing he was back in that bad situation. He would gladly inflict those sorrows and worries on himself, just to be next to Charlie. Charlie had been with him since his first day of school. He had stood up for Sticks, fought his corner, had been his true friend. Sticks let the soil fall from the shovel and turned to follow the congregation now leaving the graveyard. He rushed to catch up with the large crowd. As he got to the gate he turned to look back at Charlie's headstone. He realised his corner was now empty.

Chapter 14:

━━━

Wake Rendezvous

Charlie's family arranged tea and sandwiches in their local pub, as a way of saying thank you to everybody who had arrived and showed their support. The pub held memories of many a family story, tales of men and women, good and bad, from throughout the pub's history. Some of these stories contained Charlie's name, most didn't. Charlie had had his first drink in this pub.

Accompanied by his father, Charlie had tasted his first beer here at the tender age of eleven.

Charlie, Sticks and Old Bill had climbed the rear wall at the age of sixteen to try to 'borrow' a barrel of beer, forgetting how difficult it was to climb a wall accompanied by a three stone barrel. Yes, this pub was the appropriate place to sing their final farewells to a friend, a son, a nephew, a cousin, a neighbour. The small bar was crowded and noisy. Every seat was taken and every square foot of floor space was occupied.

Two new faces easily blended into the crowd without drawing attention. Old Bill, however, became immediately aware of their presence. It was Ben and Jerry from the security company. Ben, the larger of the two men, made eye contact with Bill, then approached the bar.

Bill used his elbow to nudge Sticks, then both friends set a course for the bar. Bill knew how risky it would be to be seen talking to two security officers. Fortunately, in a crowded bar, nobody took heed.

"It's been long enough." Ben opened the conversation. "The dust has settled on the money and it's time to retrieve it."

Bill looked at Sticks. Money had been the last thing on either of their minds in the recent months. They didn't have much time to think if this was a good idea or not. If they had a complaint, this was certainly not the place to voice it.

"When are we gonna do this?" Old Bill replied, making it sound like he had been in the same frame of mind as Ben and Jerry, so as to take the lead out of their hands.

"Three days from now, *four a.m* - you know the spot" Ben said.

"Two Guinness" Bill shouted to the barman who had approached inquisitively.

Moments passed as Bill processed the situation, then he looked to Sticks to see if he had any obvious objections. No such signs came Bill's way, so he replied: "We'll be there," as he leaned over the taps to take his drinks. He then turned and walked back to his seat accompanied by Sticks'. They had said all they wished to say and Bill was making it clear that this rendezvous had been inappropriate. Without making it obvious to the any member of the crowd, Bill sat and watched the two security guards leave the pub. Bill sat directly across the table from Sticks. He raised his glass, touched it to Sticks' pint, then they began to drink. Both men knew full well they were in this for Charlie.

Chapter 15:

~~

Digging 2

The four men arrived at the agreed place and time, prepared to withdraw their old loot. Both Bill and Sticks retrieved the shovels from the rear of the van and approached the site. Ben and Jerry stood waiting and this time appeared to be more prepared, dressed in dirty jeans and holding shovels they had remembered to bring.

"I suppose the less chitchat the better," Bill said

"The sooner we get it up the sooner we get out of here and we'll have to see less of each other. You'll even have enough money to buy your own private doctor and won't have to run into me, Paul" Ben replied, aiming his comment at Sticks.

Two hours passed and all four men where showing signs of every minute of that time, when suddenly Jerry's shovel stuck something solid. All four pairs of eyes meet Jerry's shovel tip.

They all helped clear the last of the dirt from the cases with a newfound energy and enthusiasm. They dragged the cases out of their newly designed trench and up to the quarry's sandy floor. All men present immediately became aware that the locks on the cases where busted open. Curiosity got the better of Sticks. Sitting in the dirt, tired from hours of digging and having freshly dragged himself and a heavy case out of the hole, anticipation and fear built as he put a hand to the cases' lid and pushed it back.

"What the fuck is going on here?" Ben shouted from over Sticks' shoulder.

"I was about to ask the same thing" Bill replied.

"Where the fuck is my money?"

"Our money!" said Bill. "And I'd like to know the same."

"That little prick of yours has something to do with this!" said Jerry. "If he's got my money and he's not really dead already, I promise I'll kill the fucker."

Sticks knew this situation was messed up. He knew Charlie very well and knew he was always scheming, scamming and planning. He questioned whether Charlie could have done this?

If he hadn't, it still seemed very suspicious.

"How do *we* know *you* haven't moved it?" Sticks asked.

"Cause I wouldn't have come to you and asked if *we* could dig it up, if I had it sitting at home, now would I?" smirked Ben.

"Well I would call it suspicious." Old Bill said. "You two boys arrived suited and shovel-ready.

Ya know, two fuckers who look like they'd never seen a shovel before, never mind own one, and they show up togged out with shovels in hand?"

Ben walked towards his car "Shit shit shit shit!" he said aloud. He gestured to Jerry to get in.

"Where are you going?" Old Bill questioned.

"I don't know but I'm not staying here with you two robbing bastards. Fuck that" came Ben's reply.

"You seem to be running outa here pretty quick for someone who doesn't know what just happened" Bill said.

Ben shouted from inside his car. "Fuck you! That little piss-ant Charlie is responsible for this, you know that. I know that!" He started the car and quickly vanished into a massive dust cloud as they sped out of the quarry.

Sticks aggressively threw his shovel into the back of the van.

"What are you doing?" Bill asked.

"Well there's no point in us hanging around here on our own, is there?" Sticks answered.

"No, but we can't leave this hole here with security money cases laying about, now can we? Suppose the police where to stumble by and decide this looks suspicious? Then what's stopping them inspecting the scene, finding a few fingerprints and wanting to ask you and yours truly a few questions?" Bill said Sticks looked defeated as he removed himself from the van where he had sat to rest.

"Yeah, I suppose" he answered in a breathy tone. The two friends, side by side, began filling in the cavity.

"Did you know about this, Sticks?"

"The money?"

"Yeah. The money, what else would I be asking about?"

"No, how could I?" said Sticks. "What do you mean, like, did I take it?"

"Well no, but did the person who did take it by any chance come to you and tell you what he was up to?"

"What do you mean, are you implying maybe Charlie was involved?"

"Why not?"

"He's dead, Bill! What would he do with it?" Sticks' replied in a tone which shocked himself and Bill. Saying those words seemed like an unwanted slap of reality.

"Yeah, I suppose" Bill looked as if he had been put back into line.

There was a long pause as the men stopped talking aloud in order to spend some time with their thoughts. Moments passed before both men, identical in time, tone and phrase sung the words

"What about Katie?"

They both looked each other in the eye. Still processing what they had just said and what it meant. Parallel thoughts ran through both friends' minds, although obviously unbeknown to each other. At the exact same time they were piecing together Charlie's possible last acts.

Charlie had a reason to take the money; Charlie knew he was going to die and had for some time now. Had he the time to plan such a deceitful death?

"There's only one way to be sure" said Bill. "Get shovelling, and when we're done here we're going to see Katie." Both friends hurried along with their shovelling process, possessed with a newly-fuelled drive and curiosity.

Chapter 16:

~~~

Question Time

Katie sat in the room she and Charlie had once shared. Tears covered her cheeks as she turned the pages in her photo album. Charlie, Sticks and Old Bill covered the majority of the pages.

Random family members, disposable friends and Katie herself filled the spaces between. Katie and Charlie's story was her responsibility now. She must continue to keep up the memory of Charlie. She felt alone and afraid. She did not know how to start the next chapter.

"Katie!" a voice sounded. She almost fell out of her own skin with fright as Sticks entered the room.

"You ok?" He walked to the couch where she sat. "I've been calling you from outside. I knocked twice. The car was outside and you weren't answering."

"Sorry, I was lost, here." She wiped her tears with the back of her hands. Sticks put his arms around her. He held her in silence for a moment. The friends took a deep breath together then broke from their hug. Sticks looked at her and smiled, he knew how much she missed him.

"Tea?" Sticks eventually asked.

"The cure-all medicine? Definitely!" came her reply, as they both headed to the kitchen.

"Hey, Katie, the reason I came by was I needed to ask you something" Sticks said nervously.

"Yeah shoot, what is it?"

"Did Charlie ever…well, did he ever talk about money?"

She looked at him strangely; her eyebrows implied she was confused.

"What?" she asked in a quiet tone, further suggesting her confusion.

"I mean, Charlie knew for a while now that he wasn't going to be here to….help you out.

Financially, I mean, in the future."

He paused to think and to pour the boiled water into the teapot. He then walked to where Katie sat at the kitchen table, all the while quiet. He used those three steps to find the words he would use next.

"Did he ever talk about how you'd manage when he'd gone?"

"No, not really. I suppose he always knew I was independent and well able to take care of myself." Pausing to pour the tea. "That, and knowing how strong my family is, I don't think he felt the need. Sticks, if this is about money, there's no need to worry. I'm doing just fine.

Sugar?"

"I'm supposed to be off it. It's bad for you, ya know?" he said, while gesturing for her to shovel the fourth spoonful in.

"Besides I got a letter this week about his will" Katie said, reassuring him that she'd be ok. "I've to go see a man about it in two weeks." She stirred his tea.

"I didn't even know he had a will, cheeky buggar. He must have set it up without telling me. I can't imagine why. He has nothing to leave anyone. All he owns is this house and both our names are already on the deeds, so....." She trailed off, running out of breath, refilled her lungs then took a sip from her cup. Sticks repositioned himself nervously on his seat. Excitement began to turn wheels in Sticks' head. Maybe Charlie *had* been up to something? Sticks thought before finally speaking up.

"Listen, Katie, I have to tell you something."

She interrupted him. "I know what this is about" she said, reading his nervous manner. "This is about Reilly's money, isn't it?"

"He told you?" Sticks shouted, almost choking on a mouthful of tea, spilling it down his chin.

"I'm not stupid, Sticks." she replied, jumping to grab the tea towel to mop up his mess.

"Do you three really think you are the secret service? I know you three better than anybody. He might have never told me, but I knew." She looked at Sticks; he appeared to be deep in thought, which was unusual for him.

"Whoa, whoa, whoa, Sticks. You don't think - are you telling me that the money's in his will?"she said, finally piecing his puzzled look with his strange questions.

"That's the thing, Katie, I don't know. I didn't even know of a will until now. We took the money not knowing there was as much of it as there was. We couldn't move it, so…" He paused. Katie's eyes where now wide, like a child being told a fairytale. She had suspected they were involved, but Charlie had never confirmed. Presumably because he would only tell her if she *had* to know. If it seemed safer for her not to know, then so be it. Now Sticks was confirming her suspicions with this story, and she was processing the thoughts of perhaps being left the entire loot from the robbery.

"We buried it." Sticks said.

Katie's expression changed to confusion. However, not for long, as Sticks swallowed his tea and finished.

"But when we dug it up just last night. The cases where empty" he stopped.

She knocked back what was left in her cup, wishing it were something stronger.

"Shit" she eventually managed to say. "Do you think he moved it? Into the will fund, mean?"

"Makes sense" came Sticks' reply. "It makes more sense than anything I could come up with when I saw the cases where empty."

Katie smiled, remembering Charlie's face. "Cheeky bastard! So what now?"

"Now we wait until that Will reading" replied Sticks. "Two weeks is good. It'll give some time for the dust to settle in the quarry. We wait it out, see if anybody notices the soil has been moved. See if the police have any questions to ask. Hopefully not and hopefully Charlie has been up to his usual tricks." He smiled, then drank the last of his tea. He looked into the empty cup and noted how it was still warm. Then he thought of his friend. Charlie had gone, but he may have had enough of an influence to have left the cup warm.

Chapter 17:

Anonymous Post

At that exact moment in time, on the opposite side of town, Ben, previously known as Steven, the security guard responsible for the Michael Reilly robbery, was dressing for work. It had just turned eight-fifteen p.m. and he dreaded his late shift. He sat into his car in a hurry but suddenly stopped, as a mundane object within the vehicle caught his eye. A simple brown envelope, with his name hand-written on the corner.

What's that? he thought. He did not remember possessing or leaving such an item in the car. His mind began to run. *I don't know where this came from or whose it is. How did it get there? Who's been in my car?* Most importantly - *what's in it?*

The questions stretched further and further as he reached for the envelope. On opening it he found, on a single page, a handwritten letter. He did not recognise Charlie's handwriting, why would he? He'd never seen it before. Not to mention that Charlie had not signed it. His interest heightened as he began to read. It contained information as to the whereabouts of the missing loot. The anonymous writer claimed to be holding it for ransom. Apparently, Ben possessed something he wanted more than money. It also contained information proposing a straight swap.

A destination and a time concluded the letter. Ben's mind was ravaged.

Who was this little bastard and how did he even know about the money? he thought in a rage.

He calmed down and began to think further. Then it dawned on him. Was this his chance to take the lot? Cut Jerry, Steven, Sticks and Bill from the equation? Could this be to his benefit? He mentally noted the date and time, shoved the letter into his uniform breast pocket then proceeded to work.

Little did Ben know and unbeknownst to Katie, Bill and Sticks that also at that exact same moment a second letter was being opened by Officer Carey of the Garda Siochana, not too far from where Ben was. This second letter was very similar in appearance and indeed in handwriting. However, its content differed slightly. This letter was again anonymous. The writer claimed to wish to remain unnamed, due to fear. The author claimed to know the persons responsible for the theft of Michael Reilly's money some time ago. Not only that, but they claimed to know the rendezvous place and time between the people involved. The letter gave a date, time and location, pin-pointing where the men could be found, and guaranteed they would be in possession of the stolen money there and then.

Officer Carey could hardly believe his eyes. He wondered whether to believe the words on the paper. He weighed up the fact that the letter could be a hoax against the fact that it could be legitimate. However, it was decided by officers with a higher pay packet that there would be a Garda presence surrounding the rendezvous point, surveying from a distance. It was decided it was worth Garda time to take the small risk.

Chapter 18:

Rendezvous

Ben stopped the car a safe distance from the stated meeting point. He looked at the clock on the dashboard, he was five minutes early. He could see the meeting point from where he sat.

He was parked on the edge of the causeway. Rain fell heavily against his front windscreen. He struggled to see out. He could just make out the beach where he should be meeting his anonymous associate. The beach appeared empty, not a sinner in sight. He worried. As it happened, he failed to identify Officer Carey and at least fifty other members of the force, camouflaged among the long reeds. This was where Garda officers hid behind the sand dunes, and several hid behind an unmarked Garda car parked further up the road. Each officer appeared ready to spring at a moment's notice.

Much time passed and still no sign of Ben's date. Ben questioned whether he should wander down onto the beach. It was twenty minutes past the meeting time. Maybe he or she was hiding down there, waiting for Ben to show his face. Ben thought it looked safe. Officer Carey crouched behind one of the larger sand dunes. He was accompanied by his entire precinct. He felt so proud. He was responsible for all of this. He had opened the letter initiating the whole operation, and thus he felt slightly more important than usual in this situation. He felt pride fill up his rain-soaked boots; self-fulfilment helped him ignore the pain in his neck he had acquired from his body's position. He listened to his senior officer relay instructions over the radio. The Guards had seen Ben's car arrive at the scene. They had questioned whether to proceed to interrogate its occupant. They resisted and decided to wait and observe the suspect's movements.

"Wait....He's moving, fellas, " said Senior Officer Reilly. "Yeah, he's getting out of the vehicle. Prepare to move on my mark. Over."

"Copy that, Sarge. Ready to move. Over."

Ben approached the beach with extreme caution. He approached the lifeguard's hut which was closed this time of year. He expected to find a face and possibly a name to match the letter's personality. He had decided this was a public place and, if for any reason he was seen, he could easily pass off his presence as innocent rambling. To his knowledge he was alone. Had it been a wind up? Perhaps Jerry had set him up to see if he was willing to cut him from the loot?

To Ben's surprise, in place of a person stood a rock, just in front of the lifeguard's hut. A long-handled shovel lay across it. Ben questioned his next move.

"What is this boy up to?" Ben asked himself aloud. Just over the dunes, Sergeant Reilly questioned: "Is this a wind up or what?"

Ben reached for the shovel. Inscribed into the thick wooden handle was one simple word.

'DIG'

Ben looked around him. This must have been a setup, he thought to himself. He looked up and down the beach several times. Empty. Cold and wet of course, but empty.

Who'd be on a beach when it was lashing down rain and in the middle of autumn? I could just walk away. I could just walk back, get in the car and drive away from all of this, but I'm alone here. I could dig and see if there is in fact anything beneath this sand?

In his head he weighed up his options. It was a chance, a gamble but it had to be worth risking. He stuck the shovel head in the sand and placed his boot on it. He stopped to look up and down the beach one more time. Empty. He had expected a reaction of some sort and if it had not come yet, he doubted it ever would. He began to dig.

Sergeant Reilly looked on in confusion.

"What's this cowboy up to?" he whispered to the officer next to him, lowering his binoculars and raising an eyebrow.

"Is that a go, Sergeant?" Officer Harvey radioed from his position on the beach.

"NO! No, wait. Let's see, let's watch this fella. See what he's up to. We have nothing on him at the moment. Let this asshole slip up, wait till he gives us something. Repeat that's a NO GO. NO GO."

Still no sign of anyone, Ben thought to himself as he dug.

Shovelful after shovelful he dug, his arms fuelled with passion and curiosity with every inch he gained. *Is there even anything buried here?*

He had been digging what he considered to be a long time. The frustration only fuelled his shovel even more. He was now down as far as his waist in a six foot circular hole, pumping in sweat and soaked to the bone from the rain. The tide had made its approach and would fill and drain his pit at random intervals. He was about to give up, when... 'CRACK!'

His shovel had hit something solid. *Another rock, maybe?* No, this sound different. He reassured himself. *That was a thump rather than a clung, this was hollow.* He cleared as much as he could with his shovel then reached down with his hands and turned his face to refrain from dipping it in the dirty water. He felt it, then dragged on it until it became free. His curiosity filled him to almost bursting point, as he leaned back and threw the heavy case out of the water pit.

Tired and nearly lifeless he sat on the edge of the pit, placed his hands on his hips and filled his lungs. He then struggled to raise his heavy legs and water-filled trousers from the depths of the watery pit. He rolled to his side and crawled to be where the case now sat on the beach. With the last of his energy he grabbed the nearest rock and raised it above his head.

'CRACK!' the case sounded, as it abruptly met with the heavy rock. Springing open, it answered all his questions. No, the writer of the letter had not set him up. Yes, there was one of 'his cases' in the hole and, much to his joy, yes it was full of money. It was clearly less than they had stolen, but perhaps Mr Anonymous had taken his cut.

"GO, GO, GO!" Sergeant Reilly radioed to each of the small units surrounding the suspect. "Move in!" he finished.

"Roger"

"Over"

"Go for Unit Two!"

A flurry of replies came back, as the entire police squad rained down onto Ben. Out of breath and lacking the energy to raise a limb, Ben refrained from running. There was no need to wrestle him to the ground, as he already lay defeated on the sand. Officer Carey was the first reach the suspect, so it was his hand cuffs which showed proudly around his wrists.

"Well, it doesn't get much better than this now, does it fellas?" Sergeant Reilly's deep voice boomed proudly. "Sonny, you've just been caught retrieving a stolen sum of money, as witnessed by almost every member of my police force. I can assure you, sonny, you're going away for a long time."

Ben hadn't the energy to respond, though internally he cursed each member of the Garda force, present or not.

Officer Carey softly whispered to a colleague: "Probably better off going away. Rather live in a twelve-by-twelve, than be on the streets when Reilly finds out he took his money" "I'm not so sure prison would be much safer. Kind of like going to a Christmas party at Reilly's house" his junior associate replied.

"Ha Ha! Yeah, he's damned either way, really" Officer Carey finished, whilst he placed his hand on Ben's head and encouraged it downward, as Ben sat into the back seat of the patrol car.

Chapter 19:

Phone call

'BUZZ'

Sticks' phone vibrated randomly around his bedside locker.

"Hello" Sticks croaked. It was Katie's voice on the other end.

"Sticks, it's here, in the post this morning. This coming Friday. Dear Mrs Charlie Moore, we are sorry to hear of your recent loss. As previously agreed with Mr Moore, there is to be a reading of his will no less than 14 days after….yada, yada…" Katie was unable to say the words death, loss or departure when referring to Charlie, so she skipped a large section of the letter.

"You and guests are invited to attend the reading on the twenty-third of September. Mr Bernard Molloy, Wills and Deeds Office, W.D.B., O'Connell Street." Katie ended with a large breath to refuel her lungs.

"Ok, that's it, then" Sticks replied, having now cleared his throat. "This Friday we find out where we stand. I'll see you Friday morning?" Sticks finished by asking.

Katie - "Yeah, Sticks. Bring Bill, won't you? " she answered before hanging up.

Chapter 20:

~~

Seven Years

Ben's hands filled with moisture. This was not a case of nerves, more a dread of an inevitable conclusion. He stood dressed head to toe in an orange jumpsuit. This uniform was completed by large black boots and shining handcuffs. The jury never once made eye contact with him until their verdict was being read aloud.

".....sentence you to seven years." A slight smirk fish-hooked on the corner of his mouth.

He anticipated a long sentence, so he could not express shock. His smirk was of gratitude to the anonymous letter-writer. Thanks to him, Ben had been sentenced for the theft of half a million, which Ben knew was considerably less than the amount of money taken that day. If the actual amount taken that day had been found in his possession, he would have been sent away for a guaranteed longer stay in prison. The company only had records of the movement of the original half-million, and that matched the amount the Garda managed to collect on the day the suspect was apprehended.

The case was closed. Badger Reilly knew it was best to stay quiet about how much money he had actually been shipping. It would only encourage further questions. Reilly had already decided to let it slip. Ben weighted up his odds. If he spoke out about the rest of the money, he would without doubt go away for longer. If he stayed quiet, he'd be out in six years on good behaviour, with the possibility of chasing down what he considered his money. He had no choice. He would grin and bear it. The judge's hammer dropped and initiated his descent.

Chapter 21:

━━∿━━

Will Reading

"Katie!" Knock knock knock! "Katie?" Sticks shouted again and rapped on the door. It opened and he almost fell in "I've been calling you for ages. You ok?" he said as he walked up the hall in pursuit of Katie.

"Yeah." Katie wiped her mouth

"Have you been sick?" putting a hand to her back.

"Yeah, it's just nerves." She brushed off the subject and continued to reassure him she was fine.

"We ready?" she finished.

"Yeah. Bill's got the van running" and he pulled the door closed behind them.

A large boardroom table rested between the three well-dressed men. Another gentleman stood, paperwork in hand and a smile on his face. He welcomed them into the room. Sticks, Bill and Katie entered the cold office and sat facing the suited threesome. The fourth man finally sat and started his speech. It seemed rehearsed and almost as if he had said it all before. Sticks was paying no attention to any of it, he was too mesmerised by the view over the gentlemen's shoulders.

The tenth floor. He had never been so high up in his life.

"To Mrs Charlie Moore I leave all my earthly possessions" the suited man with the paperwork woke Sticks from his day dream. "And all that is stated in the following list."

He paused to hold up a wad of paper work, which must have been the list.

"Charlie had a list as long as Santa!" Sticks whispered to his friends.

The three friends giggled then suddenly, stopping when the opposing end of the table looked at them dissatisfied. They resembled three school kids again. The gentleman continued when the 'kids' settled down.

"To Paul Sticklen, I hereby leave the contents of the security deposit box numbered 381 at the bank named and addressed above." Again he raised his hand, now holding bank details. He paused, almost expecting more giggling. None came, so he then continued. "To Mr William Olsen, I hereby leave the contents of security deposit box 382 at the bank named and addressed above."

By the time he came to the end of the will they were all showing signs of fatigue.

However, more importantly, there had been no talk of money. Not a single *'I hereby leave my millions to'* or a *'Please find all the money at said destination.* Nothing. Katie had received all his possessions. Sticks and Bill had received the contents of the security deposit boxes.

"A copy of the will is to be sent to each of the mentioned members of the contract" the suited gentleman finished, as he walked around the boardroom table and held the door open. He was clearly unhappy with the three friends' childish behaviour throughout the reading.

Katie, Bill and Sticks congregated back at the van in the basement car park of the high rise building.

"Now what?" said Sticks

"Not a mention of money," Katie said

"Have faith, will you?" said Bill. "The security deposit boxes might have money in them."

"Maybe it wasn't Charlie at all."

"A security deposit box can't fit that much money," said Katie. "And Charlie hardly could have strolled into a bank with a couple of million euros over his shoulder. Not without questions being asked a few questions, now could he?"

"A bank's the last place he'd have brought it," said Sticks.

"All I'm saying is have faith in our Charlie," said Bill. "He's always been two steps ahead of us, why would this be any different? There's only one way to find out." He got into the van beside his friends.

Katie and Sticks in unison said the only words needed: "Bank?"

Bill pulled out of the parking lot in the pursuit of answers.

Chapter 22:

Stork News

"Pull in here" Katie asked, pointing at a garage with a shop next to it. "I'm craving Monster Munch crisps dipped in coleslaw."

Sticks quickly answered with a smirk. "You sure you're not a man?"

"You sure you're not pregnant?" Bill quickly added and began to laugh.

"Ha ha! Could you imagine?" Katie trailed off between laughter.

Sticks had stopped smiling as he started to process his thoughts. Slowly he added the few clues he had and when he finished his equation it struck him like a clock tower bell.

"Katie, are you pregnant?" Sticks spat them out as if the words where burning his mouth.

Katie never said a word; she simply smiled and looked from Sticks to Bill as the van came to a halt outside the shop. Her look said enough.

"What?" Sticks and Bill said in unison.

Then Sticks broke off "and who can I ask is the father.....
Charlie's not even settled into his grave and you're out running
around town getting pregnant..."

"How dare you!" Still in the van, Katie crossed her arms
and rotated at the hips to face Sticks sat beside her. "Charlie's
the father."

Sticks started to smile. "When?" he said, before being
interrupted by Katie "Look, hold your horses. Let me go in
here and get my Monster Munch, and then I'll come back and
answer any questions you have." She crawled across Sticks
and out of the van, then she stopped and turned to them.

"So keep you knickers on, ok? I'll be right back." She
proceeded to the shop.

Some time passed by before Katie arrived back to the
van. Both her hands where now full of twelve bags of crisps.

"Holy crap, are you planning on giving birth to a crisp?"
Sticks asked, getting out letting her in. "Give me my bags!"

"Bags?" Katie cut him off. "Your bags? Plural? I got you
a bag and Bill *a* bag. The rest are for me."

Sticks didn't say a word, just looked at Old Bill and flared
his nostrils. He could not care less about the crisps. He had
too many questions.

"Explain yourself, young lady" Sticks joked with Katie.

Simultaneously she began to explain and open her crisps.

"Charlie and I had a night together before he got too
sick. It wasn't planned but it was magnificent. I'll cherish the

memory forever and although *she* wasn't planned, *she* will be cherished and loved forever."

"Did Charlie know?" asked Bill.

"Yeah, he knew. Not in an obvious way, but I knew he knew before I even told him."

"What did he say?" asked Sticks. Both Sticks and Bill sat looking at her with anticipation, like two gossiping school girls. Katie left them a moment in suspense and then finally said.

"He was the perfect gentlemen as usual. He went and produced a ring, and then he promised to be here for me and her, forever, whatever way he could…..and…"

"And?" Both Bill and Sticks asked, urging her to finish.

"And he asked if we could call her Jenny. Jennifer," Katie finished with a smile.

The two boys smiled back and each took a large breath and finally made an involuntary sighing noise. They both knew Charlie loved her. They both knew how unfair it was that Katie and Charlie had been separated. Bill started the engine and pulled the van out of the garage, headed for the bank.

Chapter 23:

Box of Tricks

Pulling up outside the bank, the excitement was building among the three friends. They looked giddy with anticipation. Were they about to find the loot in their new personal deposit box? That thought baffled them all individually.

"Ok guys, let's keep it together" Bill said, straightening his jacket. "Let's at least try to look like we own that much money. In case it is in there, I mean."

The three friends now stood side by side outside the bank. Shoulder to shoulder in unison, they all stepped into the lobby together.

"Pick one." Katie motioned towards the three queues. The three friends each joined a separate queue to speed the process along. *To cover all the bases,* as Bill put it. Sticks appeared clearly agitated.

"Will you relax? It might be nothing at all." Bills' queue moved the quickest and as he reached the desk he was instantly joined by his two friends. Having leapt from their queue, they joined Bill.

"Oooh!" the tiny lady at the counter jumped back with the fright of having her entire window filled with faces.

"Now, how may we help you today?" she said when she'd composed herself.

"Yes. Hello I'd like to view my personal deposit box please. Ashling" said Bill after reading her name badge.

"Certainly Sir, if I could just see the details of your deposit box and two forms of identification, please Sir."

Bill slid the necessary details, including the papers the will people had given him, his driver's licence and passport under the glass. He smiled, remembering he needed to seem innocent. Without giving Ashling a second to react, Sticks had stuck his identification under the glass on top of Bill's.

"Me, too" Sticks said. "I'd like access to my deposit box also, please. Ashling?"

Ashling smiled back sarcastically.

"Would you two gentlemen like to enter together?" she asked.

"Me, too" Katie blurted out. She then smiled, hoping she hadn't come across as rude.

"Of course, together all three of you." Ashling led the three friends to the deposit room after checking all three of their identifications with her manager.

"Now Sirs and Madam, if there is anything you require, please press this button for assistance." She pointed to a blue button beside the door, which was chest height on the wall inside the deposit room. Ashling, now holding both Sticks and Bills' keys, removed the two security deposit boxes from the wall. She placed them on a large table top in the centre of the room.

"Now, Sirs" Ashling finished, while handing both keys back and leaving the three friends alone.

Sticks, Bill and Katie all stepped to the table and paused to look into each others' eyes.

This was it. Was the money just inches away from the three friends? Had Charlie really gone back and moved the loot? Bill took a large breath inwards. "No matter what, we're in this together."

Sticks and Katie both took a second then responded with a simple nod. Bill released that same breath as he turned the key. He slid the lid open, only to have his view of the contents blocked by Sticks' head poking in to see for himself.

"Get outa the way."

"Empty! " said Sticks.

"Get outa the way! What? Empty?"

The box was predominately empty, save for a small brown envelope. Bill placed his hand to the back of the box and pulled it out.

"I swear to God, if this is some sort of treasure hunt, I'll kill the bastard." Bill ripped the envelope open impatiently. He opened out a letter, typed on very official-looking paper.

"What is it, Bill?" asked Katie.

Both Sticks and Katie stood wide-eyed, waiting for a response.

"It's membership to *The National Arts and Artefacts Society of Ireland*" murmured Bill.

"The what?" asked Sticks.

"*The National Arts and Artefacts Society of Ireland*" Bill repeated, sounding puzzled.

"What's that?"

"Fucked if I know." Both of them looked to Katie for reassurance. They hoped she could shed a little light on the matter.

Don't look at me, I've never heard of it either," she said.

"What are you up to, Charlie?" he said, projecting his voice up towards the roof. "Maybe yours makes mine make sense" he said to Sticks, while scurrying around to the other side of the table, where Sticks stood directly in front of his deposit box. Sticks took a breath.

"This is it. No matter...." Sticks began to mirror Bills previous speech before Bill interrupted.

"Yeah, yeah, yeah. All for one and one for all. Open the box" Bill said.

Sticks opened the box and slid the lid back. He initially resisted from reacting, then raised an eyebrow and began to smile. He reached into the box and slowly raised his hand in front of his face, holding......a brown envelope. It was identical in size, shape and colour to Bill's.

Without saying a word they all knew it must be opened. Sticks did so and soon declared:

"I am the proud owner of lot number 831!" There was a silence in the deposit room.

"What's a lot 831? Is that like a car or something?"

"No, it's not a car" answered Bill.

"What is it?" asked Katie.

"Yeah, what is it?" echoed Sticks.

"Fucked if I know." Bill was still puzzled.

"What are you up to, Charlie? Are we over-thinking this, or is Charlie two steps ahead of us?"

"Charlie has always been two steps ahead of us." Sticks continued "I don't see why dying should stop him from outsmarting us."

"Hang on, I have an address here." Bill read his letter in more detail, now that he had calmed down from his initial impatient excitement.

187 Priors Court Woods.

Quarry Estate

County Louth

Ireland

This was the heading on the top of Bill's letter. He had failed to see it first time around while rushing to read the body of the letter. He read slower, calmer this time. The final paragraph read:

"As a new member, you are cordially invited to our opening ceremony for the new season".

Bill read this aloud before trailing off mumbling to himself. Sticks stood next to the door and pushed the blue button.

"What are you doing?" asked Katie. "You're like a child."

"Well, we're done here, aren't we?" Sticks protested, looking to see if Ashling the Cashier was on her way back.

"Yeah I suppose. Where is she?" Kate asked.

"What now, Bill?" asked Sticks.

"Now we attend the National Arts and Artefacts Society's opening ceremony and try to piece together the next piece of Charlie's puzzle."

Ashling arrived back to the door of the safety deposit box room. "You require assistance?" Bill and Sticks started to clean up their deposit boxes and began to leave.

"No. No assistance thank you, just notifying you we're finished here and we'll be heading off now." Katie tried to excuse Bill and Sticks' rudeness, as all three friends rushed out the door.

Thank you" Katie finished with a bow. The three friends proceeded to the van parked outside.

Jumping into the van, the three friends all stared out the front window with expressionless faces. Every so often an eyebrow would rise on one of their faces. An idea that would inevitably run to no conclusion and the brow would lower again. They could not figure it out. They could not pin down Charlie's plan. Had he planned all of this? He always had a plan, didn't he?

Chapter 24:

Diamonds Aren't Forever

"It doesn't make sense." Sticks said what he was thinking.

"What doesn't make sense?" Bill answered him, and then continued without giving him the chance to answer. "It makes perfect sense. Charlie didn't have anything to do with moving the money, simple as that."

Katie, Bill and Sticks were sitting in Katie's kitchen. Katie was keeping busy as usual, making a large pot of tea for herself and her friends. Bill and Sticks sat at the kitchen table, arguing their minor debate. Katie approached the table holding the hot tea pot and placed it in front of Bill.

He momentarily caught sight of the ring Katie wore.

"Is that the ring Charlie gave you?" Bill questioned.

"Yeah" she replied, smiling at the thoughts.

"Where do you suppose Charlie got the money to buy a nice ring like that?" Bill scratched his head.

"How much does a fancy ring like that set you back?" Sticks followed up Bill's questioning when he realised where he was going with this. Katie looked down at her hand, which seemed complete with such a fantastic piece of jewellery.

"No. Couldn't be, could it?"Katie asked Sticks. She sounded unsure of her own question.

"Could Charlie have really spent all the money on my ring?" She began to wonder.

"No that would be a waste. Charlie knows I love him and that an elastic band to wrap around my finger would have been enough to represent our bond. The value of the ring would never have made a difference, Charlie would have known that."

"Exactly!" Sticks exploded with excitement.

"Charlie knew you would have not relied on that ring to remember him, nor would you have needed that ring in the future to remember him!"

"What?" Katie whispered, trying to predict were Sticks was going with his speech. Sticks looked her in the eye and began vocalising his thoughts as he was processing them.

"Charlie knew you loved him and would not need that ring to remember him. Maybe Charlie knew you so well that he *did* retrieve the money. He spends it on that ring, knowing that a ring wouldn't be suspicious. Knowing the police could search all of our homes if they wanted and that ring would walk out past them, under their noses, on your hand every time. Now, bear with me, he knew your lack of attachment to something material like that would make it easier for you to sell or return that ring. And you could eventually have the money, legit! He could provide for you and Jennifer without ever being here and without you having to worry." Sticks paused for a response. Katie looked back at him, her eyes glazed over. Sticks could almost see her brain adding up all of his previous words. He'd seen the moment she reached her logical conclusion, before she even said a word.

Her face illuminated. It all made sense. It did seem so like Charlie, always planning scheming.....stealing? There was only one way to be sure.

"Sticks, where could we get this ring valued?" Katie finally answered. Sticks smiled.

He seemed reassured that his previous babbling had not been wasted. He had spluttered out his thoughts without thinking them through, as usual. However her response had given him a new confidence in his compulsive story-telling.

"I know just the guy and just the place."

Chapter 25:

―᷍᷍᷍―

Got your Back

The friends looked fresh-faced. A night's sleep and a shower had done each of them a world of good. They sat in their usual positions within the familiar surroundings of the old work van's interior.

"Who is he and how do you know him again?" asked Katie.

"He's a guy who does this sort of stuff" Sticks replied.

"Yeah….but what I'm saying is…is he also a guy who does other stuff? Is he legit?"

"Yeah! How dare you, all my associates are legit!" said Sticks.

Bill and Katie smiled then giggled a little at Sticks' reaction. They could both see Sticks' excitement as he shifted around the van. He felt good. He felt like he was doing Charlie proud.

"He's a guy me and Charlie got to know at all those antique auctions, you know - penguin suit, dickie bow, a bit *la-de-dah* but a nice guy. He used to do all the pricing at those auctions. I remember because he'd tell me how much I'd usually just broken."

"Ah yeah, I remember him, nice guy" added Bill.

Where?" Katie questioned simply. She knew full well that no more words were needed in the comfort of friends.

"At one of them auction house in Wicklow later today. I gave him a ring last night and he says he has a thing happening there today and if we call down he'd have a look for us."

"Ok, I'm just still not sure of this." She looked down at the hand sporting the ring. She rubbed her slightly swollen stomach.

"You ok? Pain, cramp, what is it?" asked Sticks.

"Yeah just every so often I stop, remember and think about this baby," said Katie.

"Jeni you mean? Don't forget he called her Jennifer. He knew her. Don't you worry about that and don't you worry, she's going to know him. I'll make sure of that."

Katie smiled at Sticks' stubbornness and kind heart.

"And don't you think she'll be without a daddy. She's going to have two daddies, right Bill?" he finished matter-of-factually.

"Right about that." Bill smiled. "There'll be nobody picking on our little girl, nobody taking her dolls. Oh, and no going out in miniskirts. No boys in the house after six o' clock, no learning to drive without me by her side. No marriage unless *he* asks for my permission first"

Bill joked as he gave Katie a quick run-through of her child's life.

The three friends giggled. Katie continued to rub her stomach and smiled to herself. She knew baby Jeni and herself would both be ok because her friends had her back - and her front, for that matter.

"This is it here." Sticks pointed to a gap in the bushes which channelled both sides of the old country road.

"Here, here. On the left." Bill slowed the van down and turned in to the opening, revealing a massive pebble driveway which lead to a big Georgian house.

"Ah, yeah. I remember this place." Bill's memory came back to him as he caught sight of a large stone nameplate in the corner of his eye.

National Arts and Artefacts Society of Ireland, established 1981.

Entering the massive doorway and walking into the wide open plain that was the hallway of the house, Katie's mouth was ajar. She could not believe the house's size and grandeur. Bill and Sticks hardly reacted, they had seen all this before. They had come for business and the anticipation of finding the true value for the ring motivated them to hurry through the hall. They could hear voices, enough to be a small crowd.

The main door had been open on arrival. Nobody had yet greeted them and the car park had been full. All clear indications were that some event was taking place. Katie started to explore the hallway with her eyes. When she was happy with her findings, she then leaned around the corner to where the crowd noise was coming from.

"Master Sticklen and Master William, so good to see you two again" said the butler.

The main hall was littered with paintings. The upper-class tone was unmistakable to Sticks as turned with the fright.

"Alfred?" Sticks called back, holding his arms wide, suggesting a hug. The gentlemen's name was in fact George. However they had both become accustomed to Sticks referring to him as Alfred. This was on account of how much George reminded Sticks of Batman's butler.

"Master Sticklen, William, I am so sorry to hear of your loss. Losing a friend is not easy.

Master Charlie had always been a complete gentleman and I assure you our thoughts are with all who knew and loved him" said George.

Bill and Sticks smiled at Katie. The last time they were in this house, Charlie was with them. This was hard for the boys to consider, but less so for Katie. She was used to people telling her good things about Charlie and these walls held no sentimental value to her.

This is our friend, Katie. Katie, this is George - or Alfred, as we call him." Bill eventually fought back the tears to introduce the two strangers. He refrained from explaining her connection to Charlie, just in case George made fuss.

George or Alfred had a way with words and Bill was already close to tears. The last thing he needed was for Alfred to start telling them how magnificent Charlie was. It would start the waterworks all around.

"Katie?" asked George. "What a beautiful name. Kathleen? Kathryn?"

"It's from Kathleen but Katie is fine. Katie is what everybody calls me."

"Kathleen, Katie both are beautiful and of course a beautiful face to match. It's a pleasure, Madam," said George.

"Thank you." Katie started to blush.

"What's happening here today?" Bill questioned George, punching him in the shoulder in a sibling manner. George almost fell over from the light punch, clearly unaccustomed to such mannerisms.

"Today is the annual opening ceremony auction and ball for our *National Arts and Artefacts Society*. A fantastic occasion, we hold it every year, hence the annual term."

Katie was defying gravity; she was leaning way past a ninety degree angle to allow herself to see around the corner of the hallway. She was squinting furiously to see into the room at the end of the corridor. From what she could just make out, the room housed a crowd. A crowd almost calling Katie's name. Sticks was walking around at the bottom of the double staircase.

Looking up around the walls which held the paintings that Charlie and he had carried from the van. Reminiscing about his friend, he found himself fighting back the tears. A smile appeared across his face. Charlie never failed to make him smile.

"Would Sirs and Madam care to join or participate in our ceremony?" asked George.

Sticks snapped out of his day dreaming. "Participate? In what?"

The friends simultaneously looked at George.

"Our auction. You are more than welcome to sit in on our auction. And to purchase - if an item does so tickle your fancy" George said, raising his voice on the word 'fancy'.

"Ah yeah, said Bill. "We'll sit in and see what it's like. I doubt we'll be buying anything, though."

"Doubt we'll be affording anything, you mean."Sticks whispered to his friends as they followed George towards the crowded room.

Chapter 26:

Going, Going, Gone

The three friends immediately felt uncomfortable as they entered the room. The large crowd were all very formally dressed, and most were holding wine glasses. Bill, Katie and Sticks each looked at each other. They were dressed in what could be described as rags, at least in comparison to the other guests. They quickly took to their seats in the hope that sitting would draw less attention to themselves.

'BANG BANG BANG'

The wooden hammer echoed around the large old room.

"Ladies, gentlemen, if you could be as kind as to take your seats, our opening auction will begin" George said loudly, having hiked the three steep steps to the stage.

The three friends adjusted themselves in their seats to find comfort, as the more upper class guests slowly filled the surrounding chairs.

"Our auction shall begin with a splendid piece. Lot Number 176 is a limited edition, a Cartier gentlemen's time piece. Pocket watch. Dated 1839, it remains in near perfect condition. It completes the Cartier Series 2 Collection - and any watch collection, for that matter.

Ladies and Gentlemen, we'll open the auction at seven hundred and fifty thousand euros."

"One million euros" a strange man with a large moustache, who sat beside Katie, shouted out.

"One-point-two million!" immediately sounded form somewhere across the room.

George was pointing at every corner of the room as the voices all came together to cause a hum of random numbers being shouted. The three friends looked amazed at the amounts they had heard, before they lost track of the current offer. Suddenly 'BANG!' the hammer dropped and George shouted: "Sold to the gentleman at the back of the room. Number Thirty Six, for two-point-five million euros. Thank you, Sir. Congratulations."

As small round of applause concluded the show and the next item was quickly ushered on to the stage.

"Now, ladies and gentlemen, we have…."

He began to introduce the next item as Katie leaned in to whisper to Bill and Sticks.

"Two point five million?" Her eyes stretched open and her nostrils flared as she spoke.

Bill and Sticks both currently sat arms crossed, so to not be mistaken as a bidder with a simple gesture. They looked less surprised than Katie. They had, after all, been around these goods and others like them before.

"Sold! Sold! Sold!" each shout followed by a 'BANG' of George's wooden hammer.

There had to have been seven or eight items sold now, Katie thought. Mr Monopoly here on her left had bought at least three or four.

Then out it came. A pale cream tea pot. It was simple, yet tacky. A full row of chickens marched around its belly and a larger rooster proudly stood on top. To Katie it meant nothing, but Bill and Sticks were cast back to Charlie's admiration for the tea pot. The boys knew that this was the first of the batch of items they had most recently shipped for the auction house. Without saying a word they looked at each other.

Bill suspected that watching the next few items would be like a small slide show of when they last worked within this house. A time they had shared with Charlie. Sticks simply smiled at his friend, almost as if to say 'I'm here for you, buddy.' Bill and Sticks heard the hum of numbers erupt as before. Then time seemed to slow down and speed up simultaneously. People's mouths where moving extremely fast, like in an old black and white silent movie. However their sounds did not appear to match their movements, as muffled long-drawn tones met the boys' ears. They both felt heavy in their own bodies. Their vision appeared blurred, when suddenly.

'BANG!'

"Sold!" The little wooden hammer returned both Sticks and Bill to reality. Their senses appeared to be working as usual again.

"Come on" Katie said, nudging Sticks' elbow to encourage him to get up. She could not get past him because the gap between the seats was so narrow.

"What?" Sticks sounded confused. The boys had daydreamed through the entire second half of the auction.

"Come on. Get up. I need a wee" Katie said as she shuffled in her seat. The crowd began to stand and congregate in small groups to talk about the result of their auction. Bill and Sticks both stretched to try to shrug off their stiff tiredness. Katie proceeded to the bathroom as Bill and Sticks stood at the back of the hall. They each took a moment to recall Charlie. This whole house reminded them of him.

"Master Stickle, William. I've just been preparing the items backstage. Finalising things for both the old owners and the new owners of today artefacts" George said, walking towards them.

"And I bet you're happy with your sale. You may be better at this than you ever expected, or perhaps it's beginners luck. Could you join me to finalise your sale?" he finished, gesturing to small room adjacent to the auction hall. Both Bill and Sticks appeared glued to their spots on the carpet. They were looking confused and inquisitive. Katie returned from the bathroom and approached them from behind.

"Ready?" she asked, placing her hands on the two boys' shoulders. Without so much as a turn of either of their heads, Bill responded.

"Yeah. Could we just hang on one more minute? This might get interesting."

He followed George's lead into the next room. Sticks looked to Katie and they both followed Bill's footsteps.

Chapter 27:

~~

The Price is Right?

Once within the room, George sat himself behind a large oak office desk. The desk top was covered with paperwork, not scattered but neatly piled. The three friends sat facing the big desk. Bill and Sticks knew George well enough to trust him. They both knew if the Gardai were to find the friends in possession of Reilly's money, and if they tried to trace the three friends' movements, there was no way they could connect three working-class people with such an upper-class auction house. Even if the Gardai did, George was trustworthy.

"Yeah, like I said on the phone, we've really no idea of its value. It could be millions and it could be nothing. Hopefully millions!" said Sticks. "But either way we knew you'd have a good idea on its price, so if you could help us out we'd owe you one big time."

"Yes this ring you spoke of I, forgot about that." Alfred said. "Would you like me to have a look at the piece before we go through the details of today's sales?"

"Yeah, first look at the piece" Sticks was excited and wanted the ring valued as soon as possible.

"Why would you go over today's sales with us, what would we care about today's sales?"

Sticks interrupted Bill's questioning. "Yeah, price it first because we're kind of in a hurry" he said, trying to calm his own excitement. "Like I say, it could be millions."

"Millions?" asked George. "You say, and am I correct in thinking, it would be in my best interest not to ask how two gentlemen in your circumstances came into possession of a ring to the value of....millions? Provided it *is* worth millions, that is."

"Ah yeah you know - don't ask, don't tell." said Bill.

Katie looked at Bill and Sticks, worried.

"Nobody got hurt" Sticks assured George. If they seemed crooked, they were never the type to harm another person. George just giggled. He was a butler, remember, his family had been working-class and they'd had it hard, albeit a few generations before George's time. He understood and placed what looked like a tiny telescope on one eye, squinting to hold it in place. He placed his open hand on the table top, requesting the ring in a simple gesture. Katie slid the ring off and placed it in his palm. She never took her eyes off it, once it was out of her reach.

George looked through the tiny telescope at the ring. He held it up and looked, he held it down and looked. He let it go and placed it on the table and looked again. He took the telescope down from his eye and smiled at Katie.

What is it?" Katie asked. "Is it valuable?"

"Yes it's valuable," said George. "It is a beautiful ring and what it represents is valued above all amounts of money." George realised that this ring was bought by Charlie. George had spoken to Charlie some time ago about how to spot a valued piece of jewellery. Charlie had bombarded him with questions a short time ago. George felt proud as he realised Charlie had listened to his advice, and had selected a beautiful ring and a beautiful would-be wife.

"Yeah, but money-wise." Sticks was impatient.

"Money is of no importance for a piece with such meaning…."

"Yeah, but if you were to value it." He slightly raised his voice. Katie smiled at George's words.

"There would be no need…."

"George, we really need this ring valued."

"Yes, of course. Its price is roughly…" He looked again before finishing "….within the values of twenty to twenty-five thousand."

"Thousand?" There was a silence within the room. George looked at the three friends as they sat facing him, gob smacked.

"I'm sorry; I don't understand. Is everything ok? Did I say something wrong?"

"What? Can't be!" said Sticks. "Look again, it can't be. Look again."

"No George, it's ok. You didn't do anything wrong. We did." Bill turned to Sticks to try and calm his friend. "We were wrong, buddy. It's ok, we were just asking too much of Charlie.

It's ok." He placed a hand on Sticks' shoulder.

They looked to Katie, to see if she need needed consoling. She seemed disappointed yet somewhat happy. Sticks presumed this was due to the fact that she did not have to part with the ring. After a few moments George spoke to break the confusing silence.

"Would now be a good time to go over the sales for today?"

"You said that earlier. What about the sales?" asked Bill.

"Well, we had a good day and I thought you might like to hear the results and your estimated take-home value." George said.

"Our take home value?"

Chapter 28:

The Trail Ends?

George placed the smallest glasses any of the three friends had ever seen on the tip of his nose.

He began to read:

"Now, Master William Olsen, as Member Number 239 you are legally accessible to participate in any of the house auctions as buyer or seller. And Master Paul Sticklen as official registered owner of Item Number 831, and acting as Master Olsen's business associate, I am obliged to inform you of the sale of said item in today's auction."

He paused and looked out over the tiny glasses at the three friends, who had again taken refuge in the seats facing the desk. He continued: "If you would be so kind as to sign here, here, here and initial here, I can begin the process of fund transfer."

"Fu….fu….fu…fund transfer?" All three of the friends replied in a manner which appeared previously practiced.

"Yes, transferring the funds." George repeated, gesturing to the points on his form where the signatures where required. Would you like to meet the new owner of your item?" Alfred finished.

"My item? Funds? I own something that was in the today's auction?" Bill questioned, still confused.

"Why, yes of course! I see it was purchased in Master Charlie's name" George realised as he read his files more deeply. "Was it a gift that Master Charles bought?"

"Ye…Yeah a present. You know Charlie. Joker….." Sticks mumbled.

Bill interrupted him. "What did he own?"

George replied by holding a photograph of *their chicken teapot* as he called it. "Item Number 381."

Bill mumbled to his friends and himself. "The fucker bought the feckin' chicken."

Bill then questioned Alfred with excitement. "How much did it sell for?"

"Weren't you paying attention?" he questioned sarcastically, knowing full well auctions where not Bill's forte.

"Selling price one million euros without deductions, would you like to meet the buyer?"

"One…milli…" Sticks stuttered.

"Deductions?" asked Bill, being the more business-minded.

Sticks turned to Bill, placed a hand on each of his cheeks and pulled his face in for a kiss on his lips. Sticks then threw his hands above his head and yelled.

"One million euros!"

Katie and Sticks both jumped up off their seats and began dancing. They linked each others' arms and turned in circles, changing direction every four seconds or so. Bill mellowed after his kiss. He began with his own solo shuffle of happiness, then he joined the linking dance with the others.

"One!"

"Million!"

"Euro!"

"Oh, can I take it you were not expecting so much?" George said as he realised he was in fact talking to himself. All three friends were distracted.

"The buyers?" George directed at Bill when he eventually made eye contact.

"No thank you Sir, I have neither the need nor the desire to meet the new owners" Bill replied on behalf of Sticks, Katie and himself.

"Some people become attached to their items and wish to make sure they are going to a good home you see….No? Very well." George sighed.

Then he held the paper work above his head. The three ceased dancing to allow Sticks to sign. As requested, Sticks began filling in a form for transferral of the funds to his account. As Sticks navigated his way through the form, Bill and Katie took a moment to compose themselves. Bill held both Katie's hands and smiled.

"He did it, two and three steps ahead of us every time. The police. Steven, alias Ben. And Jerry, of course. And

Michael The Badger Reilly. That boy was special" Bill said.

Katie smiled back as a tear found its way down her cheek. She thought of Charlie being as sick as he was, he must have spent months planning this. It must have been so hard on him to deal with everything. She tried to recall, had she always been understanding? She hoped so.

Sticks walked from the table to join his friends.

"Finished." he declared proudly.

George's voice came from over Sticks' shoulder as he faced Katie and Bill in the corner of the room. "Now, if Sir would kindly give me the password to your account, I can complete the fund transferral?"

Sticks turned on his heels. The three friends all now faced George. Each of their mouths opened wide.

"Password?" was the reply from the mouths of Katie, Bill and Sticks in unison.

"Wha...wha... which...which one would that be now?" Bill finished.

"THE password? All our fund transferral accounts are voice-activated by myself, on the basis that each client possesses their own password, unknown by anybody but the client" explained George. "It helps prevent loss of any sort, you see. You can't trust anyone these days, gentlemen.

"And lady!"

"Right. That one" he looked at Katie and Sticks for suggestions. They were both frozen to the spot. *We were so close,* Sticks thought to himself. *What is he playing at now?*

Bill questioned Charlie's actions within his head.

"This is just like Charlie, do you know that?" said Sticks. "We can't just have this money; we have to deserve it, even if it's only a small amount of work. He wants us to work for it, to prove ourselves."

"Katie. It's Katie" said Bill

"I don't know, don't ask me" Katie said.

"NO! The password is Katie. Try Katie" Neither Sticks nor Katie seemed to have any objections to Bill trying it. It was worth a shot. George leaned down to the laptop and spoke the word:

"Katie."

"PASSWORD INCORRECT. PLEASE TRY AGAIN." the computerized voice answered. The three friends panicked and huddled together.

"Family?" Bill opened the debate for suggestions.

"Life?"

"God?"

"Mam?"

"Friends?" The three looked at each other on hearing Sticks' last suggestion.

Bill, Katie and Sticks opted for Friendship. Again, George spoke the word "Friendship" in his upper class tone.

"PASSWORD INCORRECT. PLEASE TRY AGAIN.

TWO ERRORS RECALLED. ONE ATTEMPT LEFT

TO CALL CORRECT PASSWORD."

This was the reply in the now almost-familiar computerized voice. Bill and Sticks started to pace the room in separate directions, each scratching their heads.

"Mam? Dad?"

"Home?" They both desperately tried to guess what Charlie might have been thinking at the time.

"Heh!" Katie cleared her throat. The room immediately went silent. All eyes were on

Katie. Did she have it? Did she know Charlie well enough to know the single word out of all the millions he could have chosen?

"Try….Jennifer?" she finally said after a long pause.

Bill and Sticks did not know whether to feel excited, confused or pensive. They would not even dare to object to such a password suggestion. George leaned over the laptop for the third and final time, and then he spoke.

"Jennifer." His unmistakable voice was rounded off by that computerized voice.

PASSWORD IS CORRECT. YOUR FUNDS ARE NOW BEING TRANSFERRED.

THANK YOU, MR STICKLEN. HAVE A GOOD DAY.

Katie placed one hand to her stomach, looked up to the ceiling, and said…

"We're going to be ok, boys."

Charlie had had a steady girlfriend for about 17 years. That figure was an estimate because Katie, the love of his life, had known Charlie since they were kids. She had grown up on the same streets as Charlie and his two best friends. She had climbed the same trees as them, known the same hiding places. She had tormented the same neighbours. They had been friends for as long as they could remember. Neither could remember a time when they were not friends. Nor could they remember a time when they were not boyfriend and girlfriend. Maybe there was no starting point, it just must have always been.

The End